If Derek Kane thought a mere kiss would scare off Stephanie Maguire, he was wrong. Very wrong.

He didn't need to know that kiss had made her stop and ponder more than once. In fact, thoughts of Derek had disrupted her work all day long. The kiss hadn't caused her to back off, however. On the contrary, it had only made her want to get to know him even better.

And she would find a way to do that. Soon.

Just as soon as she figured out how to win over a man who obviously didn't trust reporters. A man who'd been desperate enough to kiss her just to get rid of her.

She'd keep looking, keep searching, until she found out what was up with Derek Kane.

And in the meantime, she'd put that kiss right out of her head!

Books by Lenora Worth

Love Inspired

The Wedding Quilt #12
Logan's Child #26
I'll Be Home for Christmas #44
Wedding at Wildwood #53
His Brother's Wife #82
Ben's Bundle of Joy #99
The Reluctant Hero #108

LENORA WORTH

grew up in a small Georgia town and decided in the fourth grade that she wanted to be a writer. But first she married her high school sweetheart, then moved to Atlanta, Georgia. Taking care of their baby daughter at home while her husband worked at night, Lenora discovered the world of romance novels and knew that's what she wanted to write. And so she began.

A few years later, the family settled in Shreveport, Louisiana, where Lenora continued to write while working as a marketing assistant. After the birth of her second child, a boy, she decided to pursue her dream full-time. In 1993, Lenora's hard work and determination finally paid off with that first sale.

"I never gave up, and I believe my faith in God helped get me through the rough times when I doubted myself," Lenora says. "Each time I start a new book, I say a prayer, asking God to give me the strength and direction to put the words to paper. That's why I'm so thrilled to be a part of Steeple Hill's Love Inspired line, where I can combine my faith in God with my love of romance. It's the best combination."

The Reluctant Hero
Lenora Worth

Love Inspired®

Published by Steeple Hill Books™

If you purchased this book without a cover you should be aware
that this book is stolen property. It was reported as "unsold and
destroyed" to the publisher, and neither the author nor the
publisher has received any payment for this "stripped book."

STEEPLE HILL BOOKS

Steeple
Hill™

ISBN 0-373-87114-7

THE RELUCTANT HERO

Copyright © 2000 by Lenora H. Nazworth

All rights reserved. Except for use in any review, the reproduction
or utilization of this work in whole or in part in any form by any
electronic, mechanical or other means, now known or hereafter
invented, including xerography, photocopying and recording, or in
any information storage or retrieval system, is forbidden without
the written permission of the editorial office, Steeple Hill Books,
300 East 42nd Street, New York, NY 10017 U.S.A.

All characters in this book have no existence outside the imagination of
the author and have no relation whatsoever to anyone bearing the same
name or names. They are not even distantly inspired by any individual
known or unknown to the author, and all incidents are pure invention.

This edition published by arrangement with Steeple Hill Books.

® and TM are trademarks of Steeple Hill Books, used under license.
Trademarks indicated with ® are registered in the United States Patent
and Trademark Office, the Canadian Trade Marks Office and in other
countries.

Visit us at www.steeplehill.com

Printed in U.S.A.

Love…your neighbor as yourself.
—*Luke* 10:27

To my niece Stephanie—
with love always

Chapter One

◇

She was bored to tears.

Stephanie Maguire glanced up at the man sitting across from her in the posh confines of one of downtown Atlanta's best restaurants, and wondered when she'd learn to just say no to blind dates.

But this one had seemed so promising. Her best friend and the producer of Atlanta's *WNT Nightly News,* Claire Cook, had promised Stephanie she wouldn't be disappointed this time.

"He's tall, dark and handsome," Claire had told her. "And...he has a good job at one of Atlanta's hottest real estate firms. He sells property to the rich and famous. And he's pretty well off himself. I think you'll really like him."

So far, Stephanie hadn't seen too much to like. Jonathan Delmore was so self-involved that he hadn't even bothered to ask Stephanie about her own philosophy on life, or anything else regarding her life, for that matter. Why, he'd barely let her order her own food, let alone get a word in during the one-sided conversation.

So here she sat, bored and on the verge of a massive migraine, listening to Mr. Tall, Dark and Handsome—and didn't he know it—go on and on about being the top salesperson at Garrett and Garrett Realtors. If he told her one more time that he'd practically single-handedly resold every overpriced square foot of commercial property in fashionable Dunwoody to some of the richest people in Atlanta, she was going to throw her pasta primavera right in his clean-shaven face.

"So I'm definitely up for the one-million in sales per quarter award," Jonathan told her, his smile so full of self-gratification, Stephanie wondered if he even knew she was sitting across the table from him.

"That's so exciting," she replied, glad he'd let her speak at last. "But then, our work keeps us focused, don't you think—"

"That's the key—staying focused." Jonathan said, bobbing his head as he lifted his hands together to form a make-believe lens. Looking at Stephanie through the lens of his lily-white hands, he said, "And I am so good at that. It takes intense discipline—have to keep your eye on the prize." With this, he dropped his hands in a dramatic flourish and stared at her, his brown eyes boring into her as if to put her into a trance. "Focus—that's what's earned me—"

"Wow, look at the time!" Stephanie held up her left hand, squinting at her bracelet watch. "I've got to get back to the station to do an edit on a story. I'm sorry to cut our evening short, Jonathan."

Confused, Jonathan stood, watching as she grabbed her purse. "Oh, too bad. And we were having so much fun. How 'bout I drive you to the station, so we can continue our conversation, get to know each other a little better?"

Through a haze of indignation Stephanie managed a polite smile. She did not want to get to know this man any more at all. "Really, you don't have to bother giving me a ride. I'll just grab a cab."

But Jonathan, at least, was a gentleman. "Well, let me walk you out," he said. "And I need to get your home number, so we can schedule another dinner without me having to track you down at work. How about next Friday?"

Stephanie brushed a lock of brown hair off her shoulder, then shrugged. "I'll have to check my book. Reporters have crazy hours, you know."

"Really?" Grinning smugly, he added, "I wouldn't have guessed, considering it took me two weeks to finally get you on the phone. Well, you know what they say—all work and no play—"

"Gets the bills paid," she finished for him. "My

work is just as important to me as yours seems to be to you. And I'm certainly just as *focused*."

Thinking her mother would scold her for being so blunt and sarcastic, Stephanie said a little prayer for patience. She'd been raised by the Golden Rule, and while she did try to do what was right and treat others as she expected to be treated, sometimes she lost all decorum and, without thinking, let loose with her true feelings. This character flaw hadn't won her many friends, but the friends she did have understood when to back off and leave her alone.

Jonathan didn't know her well enough to do that, though. She'd have to remember that and tamp down the need to tell him exactly what she thought about him.

Jonathan hurriedly paid the tab, then turned back to her, obviously missing her little stab at his overinflated opinion of himself. "Absolutely. Staying focused, staying on top of the game, that's what success is all about. In fact, I was just telling one of our junior Realtors the other day—"

"I think I see a cab outside," Stephanie interrupted. Then without a word, she rushed out of the restaurant, intent on getting as far away from Mr. Prime Location as she possibly could.

But Jonathan was quick on his lanky feet. "Stephanie, don't be in such a hurry."

Groaning under her breath, Stephanie craned her neck, wishing for a cab to appear in the busy Peachtree Street traffic. She didn't think she could tolerate another minute of Wonderboy and his tall tales.

But no cab was in sight, so she was forced to smile at Jonathan. "Thanks for dinner. The *food* was very good."

"They know me well here," he said, winking. "And they know to treat me right."

"I'm sure."

Stephanie looked down the street again, willing a cab to appear. If one didn't come soon, Jonathan no doubt would insist on driving her back to the television station, and that might mean he'd come in to visit. Which she couldn't take.

His next words proved her right. "I'd be happy to give you a lift. It'd give me a chance to see where the famous Stephanie Maguire comes up with all those exciting, in-depth news stories."

Somehow, he sounded condescending instead of truly interested in her work. So Stephanie gritted her teeth and tried to be polite, just as her mother had taught her. "Really, that's not necessary. I'm afraid I won't have time to visit any longer tonight. I have to prepare for a story I've been working on for some time now."

"You're a very busy girl."

Groaning again at being called a girl, Stephanie bit back a retort. "Guess I'll have to call the cab company," she said instead, reaching into her purse to find her cell phone.

Just then, she heard a commotion coming from across the street. A shout echoed loud and clear through the looming skyscrapers and dark alleyways. That shout was followed by laughter and another sound.

The sound of someone striking hard against something or someone.

Stephanie looked out into the night, her eyes focusing on the direction from where the sounds were coming. In the muted glare of the streetlights, she saw shadows playing about a block away.

"Oh, my," she said, grabbing Jonathan by the sleeve of his silk suit. "Look!"

Down the street, and over, it looked as if two young men were attacking another human being. From what Stephanie could tell, the other person was also a man, but from his stooped shoulders and the way he held his arms up to shield himself, he looked much older and much more frail than his assailants.

Not even bothering to stop and think, Stephanie grabbed Jonathan by the arm, dragging him along with her as she ran toward the scene. "We have to help him," she told Jonathan over her shoulder.

Jonathan pulled at her suit jacket, bringing her to a tugging halt. "What? Oh, no. I don't think I want to get involved in a street fight. You know how those people are. We could be killed."

Shocked, Stephanie turned to stare at him, then

she heard a loud moan and the sound of a fist hitting flesh. "They're beating that man!" she told Jonathan. "We have to stop them."

Jonathan crossed his arms over his chest, then gave her an indignant shrug. "I'm not going over there. Way too dangerous."

"Then I will," she said, pivoting in a huff.

Jonathan grabbed her by the arm again. "Stephanie, it's too dangerous." Pointing to the forgotten phone she still clutched, he said, "Call 911." He backed away again. "I'll go back in the restaurant to get help."

"Okay, but I'm still going to try and scare them away."

Then she took off, dialing as she ran, oblivious to the jarring impact of her high heels hitting the sidewalk pavement, or Jonathan's cry of protest in the background. As she shouted directions into the phone to the 911 operator, telling them to send an ambulance, too, she hurried up the street.

"Hey, you, stop that!"

The thugs kept right on hitting and punching, and laughing, which made Stephanie sick to her stomach. And underneath their laughter and taunting shouts, she could still hear the moans of their victim. If someone didn't do something soon, they were going to kill the old man.

Looking around as she neared the end of the block, Stephanie didn't see anyone in sight, including Salesman of the Year Jonathan Delmore. That figured. Just another example of all the men she'd tried to date recently—all talk and no action.

Whatever happened to the good old-fashioned heroes? she silently asked herself, her heart racing as she neared the horrible scene, the moving shadows of the three appearing grotesque and enlarged on a nearby building's facade. *Dear Lord, I could use some help right about now.*

She'd just have to do something herself until the police or that help arrived. After all, she'd taken a course in self-defense and she had a pretty mean left hook from working out with the boxing bag at the downtown fitness center.

Making her way across the street until she was a few feet from the attackers, Stephanie shouted again. "Hey, I said stop!"

One of the attackers stopped kicking the old man long enough to look around at her, his eyes wild with defiance, his meaty fists raised in the air. "Yes, lady, you gonna make me?"

From out of the darkness of a nearby alleyway came a strong, deep-throated reply. "No, but I sure am."

The attacker who'd just challenged Stephanie tugged at his accomplice's coat sleeve. "Hey, man, we got company."

Surprised, Stephanie swallowed back a wave of relief and turned, hoping to find Jonathan behind her. But the man emerging from the shadows wasn't Jonathan Delmore.

He stood at least six feet tall, and from what she could see, he was built like a linebacker and dressed casually in jeans, boots and a dark leather bomber jacket. He stayed in the shadows, his legs braced apart, his hands at his sides, a deliberate calm surrounding him.

"C'mon, boys," he said, his voice even and low. "This kind of violence will only bring you trouble down the road. Walk away now and we'll forget the whole thing."

One of the youths snorted, then started laughing. "We got us a smart man here. You gonna forgive and forget, mister?"

"If you let that old man go, yes, that's exactly what I'm gonna do."

In answer, one of the youths leaned down and slapped the man lying on the ground. "You hear that, buddy? He's gonna let us beat you, then walk away."

"But we ain't ready to do that," the other youth said, coming toward Stephanie, his eyes flashing white, his hand creeping to his pocket. "We'll just have to take you down, too, I reckon."

Before Stephanie could protest, the man behind her swooped past her and head-butted one of the muggers, knocking him off his feet and up against the bricks of a nearby building. The other attacker took that as a challenge and came rushing toward the man.

But this man, whoever he was, didn't even flinch. Instead, he whirled and kicked the youth right in his midsection, sending him flying on top of his buddy.

"Want some more?" the man snarled, dancing toward the two winded, groaning people lying in a pile at his feet. "C'mon, you two, what's the matter? No more fight left now that things are a little more even?"

One of the muggers managed to get up. With some effort, he held out a fisted hand and took a weak swing toward the man. But he was too slow. The man sent him flying again with a left jab that looked like a blur to Stephanie. The attacker went down cold.

That left the other one, and he didn't seem in any hurry to get back into the fray. Trying to stand, he held up a hand in defeat, all the while gasping for breath.

That didn't stop the rescuer from taking action. "Get up against the wall," he shouted as the sound of sirens echoed around the corner. "Don't move— unless you want your teeth kicked out."

Taking a long look at his friend who was just regaining consciousness, the other fellow sank back against the wall, holding his hurting midsection. "Who are you, anyway, man?"

Stephanie wanted to know the same thing. But a

moan from the old man lying on the sidewalk sent her scurrying over to him. Leaning down, she touched his bruised and cut face with a gentle hand. "It's all right. Help is here now. Try to lie still."

As the police cars and an ambulance pulled up, she watched the stranger's face while he explained the situation and handed the culprits over to the police. He didn't even seem winded by all the fighting, and that steady, unnerving calm remained intact, in spite of the grim expression carved across his features.

She'd never seen such an interesting face. It was scraggly and dented, as if he'd seen a lot of fights such as the one he'd just entered into. His dark hair was about an inch too long for her taste, but it was thick and wavy and unkempt from fighting. She couldn't call him handsome, not in the way Jonathan was handsome. But the attraction was there, maybe because this stranger spoke of a controlled kind of power, and a quiet dignity that more than made up for his battered expression and his too-long hair.

Definitely hero material.

"Thank you, God," she whispered, her attention moving between the helpless victim and his rescuer.

Stephanie's reporter's instincts urged her to find out more, while her woman's intuition told her this man was way too dangerous to mess with.

Torn, she stayed by the hurt old man and listened

as the stranger talked to the officers in a deep-throated, lazy drawl.

"I came upon these two beating this old man," he told the policeman. Pointing to Stephanie, he added, "This lady was telling them to stop, but they didn't seem to be listening."

With that, his gaze raked over Stephanie. His intense expression bordered on anger, but there was also a resigned composure there in the crevices of his rugged features, as if he'd seen the worst of life and didn't expect it to ever get any better.

Who was this man?

She watched as he came close and stooped to help a paramedic check on the victim. As he leaned over the man, so close Stephanie could see that his eyes were smoky dark, his gaze held Stephanie's for a split second. The look was at once full of questions and dismissal. She got so flustered, she had to look away. Which really unnerved her. She didn't fluster easily.

Deciding to concentrate on the victim, so she wouldn't feel like one herself, she said, "He's hurt pretty bad."

The poor man was bleeding from a nasty gash across his forehead, and one of his eyes was bruised and swelling shut. He clutched his stomach; he probably had a couple of broken ribs. His clothes were torn and threadbare, and it didn't take long to figure out he was a homeless person, left to the mercies of the city streets, left to fall into the hands of these two young thugs.

After the paramedics lifted the man onto a stretcher, Stephanie followed them and the stranger toward the waiting ambulance. She had to hurry, however, to keep up with the conquering hero.

Wanting to know if the old man needed anything, Stephanie approached the doors of the ambulance, her gaze following the stranger who'd just come to his rescue.

"Excuse me," she said as she touched the old man's dirty coat sleeve. "Are you okay? Is there anyone I can call?"

The old man squinted, then grimaced in pain. "My money. They got my money. I had twenty dollars."

"We'll take care of that," the officer assured him. "That's pretty bad, ain't it? Young punks beating up on a helpless old man like that for a few dollars."

"Get him to the hospital," the stranger said on a snarl. Then he turned to a paramedic, his expression daring the man to protest. "Right now."

Before Stephanie could ask the man his name, another policeman came over to them. "Okay, people, tell me one more time, who saw what and what happened?"

Stephanie pointed to the two suspects now seated in one of the patrol cars. "They were beating him up," she said, her gaze shifting from the suspects to the dark-haired man who'd helped her. "I saw them from that restaurant down there." She pointed to the upscale establishment and was met with a grunt from the avenging stranger.

Frowning at him, she continued. "I shouted for them to stop, then called 911. But before you got here, Mr....?" She stopped, hoping the stranger would identify himself.

Instead, he just stood there, staring at her with that intensely dark look, as if to say, "It's none of your business, and get out of my way."

"Anyway, this man came around the corner and managed to pull them away from the victim. He was trying to talk to them, calm them down, when one of them started coming for us." She wouldn't tell the cop that the mystery man had then become like a raging bull, all fire and anger. "He saved this man. They would have killed him, I think, if someone hadn't stopped them."

The old man moaned again as the paramedics settled him into the ambulance, the stranger right on their heels.

"Don't leave yet, mister," the cop called after him.

The stranger stopped, then pivoted back around, while the ambulance zoomed away, its siren blasting.

The officer scribbled notes, then turned to look up

at Stephanie. "Ms. Maguire?" he said, recognition registering in his tired eyes. "Is that you?"

"Yes, I'm Stephanie Maguire, from WNT. Do I know you, Officer?"

"No, but I sure know you. See you on the evening news every night. My wife's a big fan, too."

"Thank you," Stephanie said, acutely aware of the stranger's dark, disapproving gaze. "Do you have any more questions?"

"Yes, ma'am," the officer said, getting back to business. "What were you doing out here, anyway?"

"I...I had dinner at the restaurant I mentioned," Stephanie explained again. "I was out front looking for a cab."

"And that's when you saw the attack?"

"Yes. I heard loud voices, then looked down the street and saw those two attacking this man."

The policeman turned to the stranger then. "And who are you?"

Silence, then a grunt. "Derek Kane."

"And you just happened around the corner, Mr. Kane?"

"Yeah," the man said, his face lost in the shadows, his hands buried in the slanted pockets of his leather jacket. "I had some business at a law office in the next building."

"Kinda late for business, ain't it?"

"My lawyer keeps long hours."

"I see. So you happened upon this attack and decided to get in the thick of things?"

The stranger let out a sigh, then lifted his head to glare at the officer. "I happened upon *Ms. Maguire* here telling them to let the man go. I was afraid they'd turn on her, so yeah, I stepped in then."

"To protect Ms. Maguire?"

"To stop Ms. Maguire from doing something stupid." The look he gave her told her that he considered her exactly that.

Appalled, Stephanie placed a hand on her hip and glared right back at the man. He had his nerve. She could have handled things. But, she had to admit, she had sure been glad when his deep voice had boomed out behind her. He had saved both the homeless man and her. She'd give him credit for that, at least.

"Thank you so much," she said on a sweet note, her own Southern drawl coming through in spite of all the diction and voice lessons she'd taken in college to get rid of it.

She was rewarded with another grunt.

Then Jonathan came strolling up, his chest puffed out, his hands on his hips, not a hair out of place. "Stephanie, everything okay here?"

"And your name?" the cop asked.

"Jonathan Delmore," Jonathan stated with his nose in the air. "I was with Ms. Maguire earlier."

"Then you saw the whole thing, too?"

"No, not really. I...I warned Stephanie to stay away. It wasn't safe. But she insisted on coming right down here. I...I went back inside the restaurant to get help."

He said this with a bit of reprimand, which only fueled Stephanie's already red-hot opinion of him. He had gone back inside the restaurant to stay safe, and they both knew it.

"He's right," the cop said, nodding his head. "You could have been hurt, too, Ms. Maguire."

"I had to stop them from killing that old man," she replied, her gaze locking with Jonathan's, and then Derek's. She refused to let either one of them make her feel guilty or inadequate for helping someone in need.

Derek Kane glanced from Stephanie to Jonathan, then rolled his eyes. The expression on his face told her everything she needed to know. He thought they were both stupid.

Thinking she'd gone from a blind date with a self-centered golden boy to running smack into the original caveman, Stephanie made another pledge to give up on the male species.

"Okay," the cop said, slapping his notebook shut. "We might need you all down at the station later for a statement. I'll need your addresses and phone numbers."

Caveman grunted again, then pulled the officer to the side. In a quiet voice that Stephanie could barely hear, he gave the officer the information he needed, which he obviously didn't think anyone else needed to know.

But years of eavesdropping on conversations had given Stephanie good information-gathering skills. Straining toward the two men, she heard the words *landscaper* and *lake,* but she didn't get the phone number or the precise address down.

Then Jonathan proudly gave his name and work number, stressing the prestigious address of both his apartment building and his work building.

Satisfied, the officer turned back to Stephanie. "Can I reach you at the station, Ms. Maguire, if I need anything else?"

She handed him a business card from her purse. "Sure. And I might need you all for comments. I think I'd like to do a story on this." She looked straight at Derek Kane then. "After all, Mr. Kane, you're a hero. You stepped in to save this man when everyone else around here refused to get involved." With that comment, she once again glared at Jonathan.

Derek Kane stepped back into the light then, the look on his face catching Stephanie and pinning her to the sidewalk. "No story."

"What? But...I have to do a story. Crime is a big issue in Atlanta, and few people want to get involved when someone is being brutalized. People need to know that there are still Good Samaritans like you who are willing to help out a fellow human being.''

He stepped closer, his face inches from hers, his eyes such a dark gray, she immediately thought about smoke and fog and the granite that formed Stone Mountain. "I said no story, lady. And I mean that.''

Turning to the police officer, he repeated all of it. "I'd appreciate it if you'd keep me anonymous, understand?''

The officer, although clearly surprised, nodded grudgingly. "If you say so.''

Derek Kane looked straight at Stephanie. "I say so.''

Shaking in her pumps, Stephanie nonetheless stood her ground. "So you're refusing to cooperate?''

"Yep.''

With that he turned and started walking away, his cowboy boots clicking against the sidewalk with precise measure.

"But it would make such a good story," Stephanie called after him. "At least take one of my cards, in case you change your mind.''

He didn't even bother turning around.

Chapter Two

Dawn was coming over Lake Lanier.

The sight never ceased to amaze Derek Kane, which was why, he supposed, he automatically woke up at this time every morning. He liked to see that golden sun coming up through the trees, its rays spreading out over the water. It reaffirmed that at least for a few precious minutes everything was right in God's world.

Maybe that was why rainy days got to him so much. That and the fact that if it rained, he didn't get much work done.

But today Derek didn't have to worry about rain. From the looks of that sunrise, there wouldn't be a cloud in the sky and he'd be able to get his landscaping and yard work assignments completed.

Taking another sip of the strong coffee he'd

brewed earlier, Derek closed his Bible and reached down past the deck chair to rub the nose of his faithful companion, a German shepherd aptly named Lazarus because Derek had literally saved the dog from being put to sleep a few years ago.

"Ready for our run, boy?"

The black-and-tan animal jumped to attention, his big tongue hanging out in a drooling acknowledgment. When that didn't bring his master to his feet, Lazarus barked and wagged his tail in the air.

"Okay, okay. Sorry I'm moving kinda slow this morning. I had a late night, you know."

Lazarus tried one more trick. He flopped down on the planks of the big deck, then rolled over for a belly rub, his black eyes filled with what he obviously hoped was sadness and despair.

"You're pathetic," Derek said, grinning as he, too, plopped down on the deck next to the dog, then proceeded to rub Lazarus for all he was worth. "How's that?"

The dog seemed content to stay that way all day.

"Now look who's lazy," Derek replied. Bringing his hand up to the dog's long neck, he absently continued scratching and rubbing the coarse fur.

"I met a woman last night, Laz," he said, knowing he could tell the dog anything and it wouldn't get repeated. "A woman I see every night on the evening news." He shrugged against the deck planks. "Actually, she's all over the place, everywhere in Atlanta, on billboards, on the sides of buses, in ads in the newspaper, a well-known face. And unfortunately, I had to run upon her near a dark alleyway while she tried to fend off two thugs twice her size."

To save a helpless, homeless man, Derek silently reminded himself. Stephanie Maguire had been trying to help a stranger. And because of that one brave act, he hadn't been able to get her out of his mind.

Not through the long, tiring wait in the emergency room of Grady Hospital, not through the endless paperwork and the necessary questions later at the police station, and certainly not through the long trip back home a couple of hours ago.

She was beautiful. Every man in metro Atlanta and the surrounding counties could see that. And they all got to view her lovely face each night as she reported the news across the airwaves. Her hair was long and wavy, fluffed out around her face and shoulders in a feminine style that somehow didn't match her hard-hitting attitude when she delivered the news each night. Stephanie Maguire always looked a little windblown, as if she'd just come rushing in off the street to deliver her piece. Which she probably had. But she delivered with precision and accuracy, her stories in-depth, her eyes wide open.

And about those eyes.

Derek knew *all* about those eyes. Blue green and big, as mysterious as the lake waters, and just as rich and full of depth. As the old saying went, a man could drown in those eyes.

But not this man. No, sir.

Derek pushed himself up off the deck, then whistled to Lazarus. ''C'mon, boy. Let's get that run started. We've got lots of work ahead of us today.''

And lots of turmoil to work off on a long, tough jog.

Derek just hoped that Stephanie Maguire would heed his warning and keep him and his so-called heroic deed off the evening news. He didn't need or want the publicity. He didn't want people nosing into his life, or second-guessing his motives.

He'd had that once, but never again.

Not even for beautiful, popular newshound Stephanie Maguire.

As usual, the World Network Television newsroom was buzzing like a well-oiled machine. Stephanie glanced around at the action—people busy talking on the phone, busy arguing with leads and checking out sources, or arguing with editors and producers—her adrenaline kicking in with each screech of the newswire, with each beep of the humming computers, with each beat of her heart.

She loved her work. Loved it with a passion that

bordered on obsession, loved it because it brought her life and hope and a sense of accomplishment.

But this morning she had to admit she was tired. It had been a late night last night. Hours after she'd left the scene of the mugging, she'd lain awake in her downtown efficiency apartment, the sounds of never-ending traffic soothing and steady way down below, wondering if that old man was all right. Wondering who Derek Kane was and why he refused to be acknowledged as a hero.

And wondering why Derek Kane had gotten to her so much.

The homeless man's name was Walter Griffin. He sometimes stayed in a shelter not too far from where he'd been attacked, but with spring just around the corner, Walter had ventured back out onto the street to sleep. And he'd been almost beaten to death because of it.

She'd already interviewed him early this morning from his hospital bed, a camera crew taping his every word. Even though Mr. Griffin could barely remember what had actually happened, he'd be all right. But he'd have to stay in the hospital for a few days due to a concussion, two cracked ribs and several lacerations to his face and hands.

Stephanie had promised to check back with him, but in the meantime, she also wanted to find Derek Kane. She needed his comments to finish out the story. And she needed to know more about him.

"You look like you're onto something," Claire Cook said as she leaned over Stephanie's cluttered desk to hand her a bagel and a latte from the coffee shop downstairs. "Your eyes are positively sparkling." Pushing lightly at Stephanie's navy wool jacket, she said, "C'mon, give it up, Maguire. What are you working on?"

"Nothing," Stephanie admitted as she tore the plastic lid off her double latte, then poured the frothy mocha contents into her favorite Do It Now coffee mug. She refused to drink out of foam cups. "Exactly nothing."

"Exactly something," Claire retorted. Scooting into a nearby rolling desk chair, she pulled up beside Stephanie, her green eyes bright with anticipation and her short red hair standing on end across her head. "I know that look."

Stephanie tore off a hunk of blueberry bagel, then sighed before popping it into her mouth. Between bites she said, "I thought I had a story—I was involved in a mugging last night—"

"Oh? Are you all right?" Claire scanned her face, obviously checking for bumps and bruises.

"I wasn't mugged, but I saw it happening. An old homeless man named Walter Griffin—these two young boys, juveniles with previous truancy and vandalism records, according to the police report, were beating him to a pulp right there off Peachtree."

"And you intervened." It was a statement, based, Stephanie guessed, on the fact that the veteran news producer knew her reporters well.

"I had to," Stephanie said, shrugging her shoulders by way of defense. "Nobody else would—including your wonder boy, Jonathan Delmore."

Claire perked up considerably, her head coming up so fast her multifaceted turquoise-and-silver earrings jingled against her slender neck. "You were with Jonathan last night?"

"For two excruciating hours," Stephanie said on a wail of exaggerated pain. "Where did you find that overblown egomaniac, anyway?"

Grimacing, Claire said, "I take it, it wasn't love at first sight."

"Not at all. The man is so stuck on himself, he could be patented as the new wonder glue. Anyway, we'd just left the restaurant, *thankfully,* and I was looking for a cab, when we saw these two overgrown adolescents mugging and beating this old man. I tried to get Jonathan to go with me to help them, but he refused! He went back into the restaurant, he later said to get help, while I called the police and screamed for them to stop."

"And then you waited from a safe distance?" The question was full of hope, but Claire's expression said she already knew the answer.

"No, I ran toward them, shouting at them. They

were kicking him and pounding him—I had to make them quit.''

Claire took one of Stephanie's hands in hers. ''You've got to stop trying to be a hero, honey. You can't save all of them, you know that.''

Stephanie looked down at Claire's dainty little wrinkled hand, covering hers. Claire wore several rings of various shapes and sizes. Stephanie focused on a bright topaz pinkie ring, unable to look at her friend's face. ''But I could see it in my mind, Claire. I could see my father all over again.''

''What happened to your father was a tragedy, Stef, but that doesn't mean you have to throw yourself into every crime that's committed on the streets of Atlanta. One day, something terrible might happen to you, and then what would your mother do?''

''I know, I know,'' Stephanie said, her bagel cold in her hand. ''And I'm careful—you know that. I did call the police last night, but I just couldn't let it happen again. Not to that helpless old man.''

Claire patted her hand, then let go. ''Okay, so what happened? Did you stop it, or did the police get there in time?''

Stephanie chewed another bit of bagel, then sipped her lukewarm latte. ''That's when *he* came out of the shadows, like some caped avenger.'' Shaking her head, she looked up at Claire at last. ''I tell you, Claire, I'd never seen anything like it. He reminded me of my father—Daddy would have done exactly the same thing.''

''Who? Who helped you last night?''

Stephanie threw down the leftover half of her bagel, then pushed both hands through her unruly hair. ''His name is Derek Kane. He's a man—''

''I gathered that much,'' Claire said, a wry smile moving across her freckled face. ''And apparently he came to your rescue?''

''He did,'' Stephanie admitted, bobbing her head again. ''He just stepped out of the shadows and told the muggers he was going to stop them and then…well, after talking to them didn't work, he rushed one of them and sent him flying. Then he turned around and kicked the other one right in the stomach. The whole exchange lasted less than a minute, and then he had them up against the wall.''

Claire blew a breath up on her spiky bangs, causing them to flutter across her forehead. ''Okay, so you two played Starsky and Hutch? So why aren't you writing the story for the noon news?''

''Because Mr. Kane refused to be interviewed.''

''That's never stopped you before.''

''He made it very clear. The man doesn't want to be bothered.''

''Like I said, that's never stopped you before.''

Stephanie shot her friend a grin then. ''No, it hasn't. That's why I'm putting together the story, with an anonymous hero as my focus. I hope we can

run it tonight at six and eleven. And in the meantime, I've got research digging to find all the Derek
Kanes listed in Atlanta and the surrounding vicinity.
I intend to track him down and find out why he
doesn't want to be in the limelight.''

"Intriguing," Claire said, maneuvering her chair
back to the desk across from Stephanie's. "A man
with something to hide is forced into the role of a
Good Samaritan, huh?''

"I'm beginning to think that," Stephanie replied.
"And if Derek Kane is hiding something, I intend
to be the one to find out what it is.''

"Tell me something, kid," Claire said, leaning a
hip against the corner of Stephanie's desk. "Was
this Derek Kane young and attractive, or old and
feeble?''

"He was...gorgeous," Stephanie blurted out before she could catch herself. Quickly she added, "Of
course, it was dark and he stayed in the shadows for
the most part, but—''

"But you're interested?''

"No, no. Not in him as a man. He was too snarly,
too..." She couldn't put her finger on it, but there
was something awfully familiar about Derek Kane,
besides the way his actions had reminded her of her
sweet father. And that something had been eluding
her all night and morning. Maybe that was why she
had such an incredible urge to find the man and get
to the bottom of his story.

"So what did he look like?"

Stephanie crossed a long navy-stockinged leg, then watched the wide pleats of her matching skirt settle over her knee. "Dark hair—kind of shaggy, leather jacket, cowboy boots, jeans...and from what I could tell...the most incredible gray eyes—deep gray."

"Wow." Claire stared down at her, her green eyes shifting like a cursor on a computer screen. "Our man Kane does sound intriguing. Maybe he's a movie extra or stunt man, or maybe even a movie star. Hollywood is always making films on the streets of Atlanta."

Stephanie shook her head. "Oh, no. This man definitely shuns the spotlight. I doubt he has anything to do with Hollywood. Maybe...maybe he's a detective! He did say he'd been to a lawyer's office nearby."

"Honey, from your description, I'd say he's dangerous, at any rate."

"Yes, you can be sure of that," Stephanie told her boss as she uncrossed her legs and pushed her chair back from her desk.

"Too dangerous?" Claire asked, rising to get on with her busy day. "I mean, too dangerous to consider getting to know on a personal level, of course."

"Yes. Tall, dark and definitely dangerous. And not my type."

"Sounds exactly like your type." Claire threw the comment over her shoulder as she waved. "Keep me posted—on the story, that is."

"I will," Stephanie promised, ignoring Claire's suggestive look. *And I will find Derek Kane and I will find out what he's hiding.*

She told herself it was all about getting the story. That was her goal, after all. To get the story, find out the truth, expose corruption, save the day.

But you couldn't save your father, could you, Stef?

No, because she'd been too young to understand how to save him, to even to begin to understand his death.

Putting those thoughts out of her mind, Stephanie looked at the Bible verse her mother, Vanessa, had cross-stitched for her the Christmas after her father had died.

"The just shall live by faith."

Romans, chapter one, verse seventeen.

Stephanie read that verse each time she sat down at her desk, but she remembered that justice didn't always seem fair. But, as Vanessa would remind her time and time again, she didn't have to depend on justice alone, as long as she had her faith, too.

"My father lived by faith," she whispered now. "And he died trying to bring about justice."

Where was the fairness in that? Stephanie had to

wonder. Her mother believed faith and justice could work hand in hand. Stephanie still had her doubts.

But it had worked last night. She'd tried to save Walter Griffin. And she'd asked God to send her a hero, someone strong and true, as her father, Donald, had always been.

But then along came Derek Kane.

A reluctant hero.

And a man she couldn't seem to get out of her mind.

Because of the story.

Or because as Claire had sensed, there was more to the story. Much more. Stephanie had to admit she was intrigued by much more than just the facts. She wanted to know what had made Derek Kane so bitter, so antisocial, so unwilling to be recognized for his good deed.

"And I won't stop until I find out what it is," Stephanie told herself as she booted up her computer. "There can't be that many men in Atlanta named Derek Kane. He should be easy to track down."

Chapter Three

Derek slowly tracked the shovel through the rich, moist loam of the flower bed he was building for Miss Nadine Hamilton. Miss Nadine, as she had graciously suggested he address her the first time they'd met years ago, was eighty years old, petite and so loaded with old Atlanta money that Derek doubted the woman even knew how much she was really worth. She came from a lineage that dated back to well before the Civil War, and her hair was a silvery blue, as blue as her blue blood, Derek guessed.

On second thought, Miss Nadine probably knew down to the penny how much money she had, since she scrutinized each and every flower, shrub and bag of manure Derek had ordered to finish her spring garden in time for the annual Azalea Pilgrimage her church group had organized many, many years ago as a means of "helping those less fortunate."

Derek liked working for Miss Nadine. She was one of his favorite clients. She kept him busy, kept him on his toes and always managed to lighten his day with her words of advice or her analysis of life in general. She could quote whole passages of Shakespeare, and whole books of the Bible, but she spoke only when she felt the need to get her message across.

Derek heard one of the tall French doors of the house opening and looked up to find Miss Nadine coming toward him. Her morning inspection of his work, no doubt.

"Land sakes, Mr. Kane—" she insisted on calling him Mr. Kane "—when did the price of fertilizer go up so high?" she called out, her tiny veined hands on her hips, her wrinkled pink face twisted in a frown of disapproval.

Derek dropped his shovel, then, to peek up at her, lifted a cluster of the ageless Confederate jasmine trailing along a pretty latticework arbor. She was standing above him on the elaborate circular brick veranda that bordered the back of her twenty-room mansion in one of the oldest, most prestigious neighborhoods in Atlanta—Buckhead.

As she petted Lazarus on the head, she pointed with the other hand to the nearby bags of fertilizer he'd picked up at the local nursery earlier. "I can't afford much more of this stuff, and still be able to pay you, too, you hear me now?''

"Yes, ma'am," Derek called, waving a hand. "I'll try to keep things under budget."

"Well, see that you do." Cooing to Lazarus, she added in a huffy voice, "And don't let this over-grown mutt mess up any of your handiwork, you hear?''

Derek had to grin. Miss Nadine knew his one stipulation—Lazarus came to work with Derek, and that was that. The dog was trained to stay where he was told. Besides, he was too lazy to go digging for bones. He wouldn't dare venture into any flower beds.

And both Derek and Miss Nadine knew that.

Even though Miss Nadine looked as stern as a schoolmarm standing there in her crepe floral dress and immaculate bone-colored pumps, he could see the twinkle in her blue eyes even from this distance. Miss Nadine liked to complain about everything from the weather to the state of the world to how broke she was, but Derek had been her landscaper for over four years now, and he knew that when he was finished, Miss Nadine would not only pay him, but she would give him a big tip to boot.

"How's life treating you, Miss Nadine?" he asked, if for no other reason than simply to hear her cultured, ladylike voice carrying out over the cool spring morning.

"Life is a constant mystery, Mr. Kane," she replied as she carefully made her way down the circular steps leading out to the sprawling backyard of her estate. "I suppose, however, that I can't complain on such a lovely day as this. The good Lord truly saved this one up for us, didn't he?"

"I believe so, yes, ma'am," Derek replied as he plucked and pruned the yellow buds of the fragrant jasmine. "I needed a pretty day, too. He sent it right on time."

Miss Nadine pinned him with her big baby blues. "Did you go gallivanting last night, young man?"

"Gallivanting?" Derek gave her a wry smile. "I think I'm too old for gallivanting, don't you?"

"Hmmph. Thirty-two and already calling yourself old? Wait until you get to be my age. And you didn't answer my question."

Derek didn't want to explain to Miss Nadine Hamilton, of the Atlanta Hamiltons, that he'd spent the better part of last night in a hospital waiting room, taking care of a homeless man who'd been beaten on the street. And he especially didn't want to explain how he'd made a special trip to the police station in the middle of the night to give a complete statement, in private and with the understanding that Derek's identity would not be made public. He had enough to worry about with Stephanie Maguire hot on the story.

It wouldn't do to tell Miss Nadine—she'd repeat

the entire story to the whole garden club before noon. *"And yes, it was my yardman, my yardman, I'm telling you, who helped the poor, lost soul."*

Derek didn't mind being referred to as a yardman. That was his job, after all, and one he took very seriously. He just didn't want Miss Nadine or any of his other clients to get wind of what had happened in downtown Atlanta last night. Because then they might find out the truth; then he might have to give up his safe, secure, anonymous life here in Atlanta and move on. And he couldn't do that.

"I had a long night, that's for sure," he told the tiny lady now. "Didn't get much sleep, but I wasn't misbehaving. Just had some things to sort through."

"Personal things, I reckon." She reached up to help him pluck the faded jasmine blossoms, her lips pursed, her expression devoid of the acute interest Derek could see in her eyes.

"Yes, ma'am. Just business. I had a meeting with my lawyer—getting some finances in order, seeing about investments and such. Left me pretty tired."

"Investments?" Miss Nadine's tiny head came up. "Mr. Hamilton, rest his soul, would have been thrilled to help you out there. He was one of Atlanta's top brokers in his day, you know. Did I ever tell you that?"

Relieved that she'd found something other than his own personal life to focus on, Derek encouraged her with a smile. "You've mentioned it a time or two. I guess he was pretty successful, huh?"

"Successful enough to leave me quite comfortable in my old age," she stated with all the dignity and discretion that befitted her stature in life. "That is, if my yardman doesn't rob me blind buying fertilizer and landscaping timbers."

Derek saw the smile curving her feathery lips, then grinned over at her. "Can't take it with us, can we now, Miss Nadine?"

"I reckon we can't," she replied, chuckling. Reaching over to pat him on the arm, she added, "You sure do fine work, Mr. Kane. I can't fault you there."

"Thank you." Derek couldn't help but feel a bit of pride. Miss Nadine rarely gave out compliments. "It's coming along just fine. We'll have it in tip-top shape for the reception to kick off the Azalea Pilgrimage, I promise."

Miss Nadine turned to head back to the house. "I know I can count on you. About a week—the azaleas will peak in early April, according to my calculations." She waved over her shoulder. "I've got committee work to attend to. Come by the kitchen before you leave. Cook will have you a bite to eat prepared, and a treat for that mutt."

"Yes, ma'am."

Derek watched as the old lady walked with straight-backed precision across the wide veranda.

She really was a sweetheart, always feeding him and fussing at him and telling him he needed "to settle down with a good Christian woman and have a passel of babies."

Derek appreciated Miss Nadine's well-meaning intentions, but he'd long ago given up on being a family man. What woman would want to get involved with the likes of him, anyway?

That thought brought him back to Stephanie Maguire. Of all the women in the world, why did she have to be the one he'd run into last night? And why had he stopped to get involved in the first place?

"I should have kept on walking," he mumbled to himself as he picked up his shovel and started slinging dirt with a fast, furious pace. "I knew better. I knew."

But Derek also knew that he couldn't have just walked away from the scene spread out before him on the shadowed street last night.

He'd left his lawyer's office, discouraged but still determined to get his life back in order, only to discover two kids—teenagers at that—attacking a helpless old man. And...a beautiful, slender woman, with nothing to protect her but a cell phone and a purse, screaming at them to let the man alone.

Anyone else would have done the same thing, Derek reminded himself.

Or would they?

He'd seen the darker side of life; he'd seen the worst the world had to offer. For the most part, there was good in the world. But when the evil crept in, it devoured everything in its path.

Derek had seen that kind of evil, that kind of despair. He'd witnessed it down to his very soul, and, soul weary, he'd walked away and found a safe haven amid trees, flowers and earth. He'd needed to find his soul again, to find his faith again, to find God again, and becoming a landscaper had helped him with that.

It had been a natural transition. He'd grown up on a farm in south Georgia, had worked the land before he'd headed off to greener pastures, before he'd taken on a job that had almost brought him to the brink of madness.

Derek stopped shoveling and looked out over the vista of Miss Nadine's tranquil garden. The azaleas stood in thick clusters underneath the tall pines, some of the bushes reaching six or seven feet in the air, their satiny green leaves bowing gently in the morning breeze, their colorful fuchsia- and salmon-tipped buds just beginning to crest open.

The grass, polished and clipped, spread like a velvet blanket out over the rolling terrain. The sun played across an ancient rose garden where bees hummed greedily over the feathery red and yellow blossoms. Way down a sloping hillside, a stark white gazebo filled with wicker furniture fat with floral cushions stood covered by dainty trailing purple wisteria vines and delicate white-tipped Cherokee roses.

The air was filled with the sweetness of hundreds of blossoming flowers, mixed with the rich smell of fresh earth and the softer, more subtle scent of still-moist dew.

Such a peaceful, gentle spot. Such a beautiful retreat. And Derek was its caretaker.

He couldn't, wouldn't lose any of this. Not the fragile peace he'd found, not the respect of his clients, not the contentment of a good day's work—he wouldn't allow anything or anyone to take that from him.

And that included Stephanie Maguire.

Derek looked up at the billowing white clouds floating by like puffs of cotton. "Lord, I've tried so hard to make a new life for myself. I've prayed and I've asked for forgiveness and I believe You have heard my prayers. Don't let it end now, Lord. Don't let them find me." Thinking of Stephanie Maguire again, he added, "Don't let *her* find me."

He didn't need a reporter snooping around, nosing into his life. Even if that reporter was lovely to look at, intriguing and definitely a woman who could make him come out of his self-imposed exile.

He was safe here, in this world of earth and sky.

He didn't want to be found, because Derek Kane knew in his heart he was nobody's hero.

And he surely didn't want the whole world to come to that same conclusion. But if Stephanie Maguire pursued her story, if she tracked him down and insisted on putting him on the evening news, that's exactly what would happen.

And his life would be destroyed all over again.

"We'll just have to start all over again, from the bottom up."

A long, low moan followed Stephanie Maguire's statement.

"Alonzo, are you complaining?" Stephanie asked, her hand pulling through her mushed hair as she leaned forward on her cluttered desk. "You know how I feel about whining, now, don't you, Alonzo? And especially from a Georgia Tech journalism student."

"Yeah, yeah." Alonzo Sullivan scratched his nose, then tossed back his short dreadlocks, his brown eyes opening wide at the woman who sat staring over at him. "I'm not complaining, Stef. Not one bit."

Stephanie sent the intern a bleary-eyed stare. "Funny, I sure thought I heard a loud moan coming from your direction."

"Just stretching my throat muscles," Alonzo replied, a huge grin cresting on his face. "But...do we really have to do all this research again? We've checked on every Derek Kane in Atlanta, haven't we? And…it is almost midnight."

Stephanie nodded her head slowly, exercising tired shoulder muscles in the process. "Do you have early classes tomorrow?"

Alonzo lifted a brow, as if debating whether to tell her the truth or not. "No, I don't have any classes in the morning, but—"

"So, you can stay and help me go back over all these printouts from the DMV and compare them to the names we've gathered, right?"

Alonzo slowly nodded. "Yeah, sure. Who needs sleep."

"I've told you a hundred times," Stephanie replied, playfully slapping the twenty-year-old on the shoulder, "reporters never sleep."

"Why did I have to major in journalism, anyway?" Alonzo mumbled. Reaching for the phone book, he shot her a steady brown gaze. "And why is it so important that you find this man? You already did the main story—without him."

"I want to interview him," Stephanie told her confused helper. "I was involved in this…mugging and Derek Kane…well, he saved a man's life. He's a hero, and I think he should be recognized as such. I think people need to know that there are still some heroes left in the world."

Stephanie watched as Alonzo started organizing all the Derek Kanes, Derek Canes and Derek Cains they'd found on the Internet and in the phone book. After comparing those to the records they'd found through the Department of Motor Vehicles, they'd called most of them, but so far, no one fit the bill of the Derek Stephanie remembered from two nights ago. But she wasn't ready to give up yet.

"This isn't your usual type of story," Alonzo pointed out as he once again went down the list. "You usually go for the more hard-hitting news."

Stephanie scanned her own list. "Yeah, well, I guess I want to interview Mr. Kane because he…he seemed so reluctant. Here's a man who risked his own life to come to the aid of someone else, yet he doesn't want anyone to know about his good deed."

"That is strange."

"Yes, and it got me curious. Plus, I just think it would make a good human interest piece."

Alonzo rolled his eyes, then pointed a finger at her. "You think there's more to this, right?"

Stephanie had to laugh. "Alonzo, you're getting too good at this job. Yes, I certainly think there's more to this. I can't get this man out of my mind."

"How about the police?" Alonzo suggested. "The officer who arrested the youths? Have you talked to him?"

"Several times," Stephanie replied. "For some reason, the arresting officer is staying mum on the subject of Mr. Kane—which makes me even more suspicious. Of course, if we have to testify as witnesses, I'll see Kane at the hearing, I'm sure. But I don't want to wait that long. This story is fresh and I want to interview him now. But the police haven't really been any help." She grinned then. "Although I do have a copy of the police report, of course. The teenagers are being held as juveniles, so they'll be arraigned in a couple of days. I don't want to wait until then, because I have a feeling our Mr. Kane might not even show up for the hearing."

"So we have to dig through all these names again?"

"Yes, we do. And call them."

"Now?"

Stephanie glanced at the clock. "It is late. Okay, we'll go back over the list and eliminate the ones we know are definitely not our man."

"Like the seventy-year-old Derek Cain who proposed to you over the phone?"

"Yes. Nice, sweet man, but not my type."

"Well, out of the twenty-two we've called, seven have asked for your hand in marriage, and about three wanted to know if you'd live in sin with them."

"None of them would be our man," Stephanie replied, ignoring the sometimes flattering, sometimes disturbing adulation she received from a lot of her male viewers. "This particular Derek Kane acted as if he loathed the ground I walked upon."

''So naturally he's the one you're going after, right?''

Stephanie grinned again as Alonzo fell back into his assigned task with no more complaints. He was a good kid, and a hard worker. He'd make a good reporter one day. Right now, Alonzo and the other interns got stuck with the grunt work, but then, reporting was ninety percent grunt work, anyway.

And she should know. She'd taken some pretty big risks just to get to a story. So going after a man who didn't want to be found was nothing new for her. Only, this man was different.

She was attracted to this man. Which was silly. She didn't know him, had barely seen his face. Yet…it was there, staring her in the face, keeping her edgy and impatient. She wanted to know more about Derek Kane, because she was interested in him.

Putting that thought out of her mind, Stephanie helped Alonzo reorganize the list, then sent him home.

Sitting there in the almost empty press room, Stephanie once again went down the list. They'd called all the Kanes in the metro Atlanta area, and several in the outlying areas. He had to be out there, somewhere.

Thinking back over that night, she tried to remember everything Derek Kane had said or done. The clues were there. She had to put them together.

"Where are you?" she asked now, her gaze moving down the list. "Maybe that's not even your real name."

She was about to call it a night when her gaze hit on one address in particular. They'd called that number earlier, but no one had answered, and there hadn't been an answering machine either, so she hadn't been able to listen to the voice. Call it a hunch, call it woman's intuition, but this address stood out in Stephanie's mind for some reason.

"Flowery Branch, GA."

Flowers? Flowers. Then she remembered—he'd said something about landscaping. Was he a landscaper?

"Think, Stephanie." Then it hit her. She'd been eavesdropping when Derek had given personal information to the officer. Now two details of that conversation stood out in her mind. Landscaper...and lake.

"Would a reclusive man who claims he's a landscaper live at a place called Flowery Branch?"

He possibly could, if that place happened to be near a lake.

Flowery Branch was a little town near Lake Lanier, about forty miles northeast of Atlanta.

"The landscaper who lives on the lake."

As she sat there, her heart picked up its tempo. One of the DMV printouts matched this address.

And the physical description matched perfectly, too. "This could be him."

But she needed to be sure.

Picking up the phone, Stephanie called the Atlanta Police Department and waited as the operator connected her to one of her most reliable sources on the night shift. If the arresting officer didn't want to divulge anything about Derek Kane, she'd just have to resort to other tactics.

"I need a favor," she explained, then after giving her friend the details, she said, "just verify this for me. Just verify that his occupation is landscaper and that his address is Flowery Branch, Georgia. That's all I need."

Stephanie hung up, then waited. If this hunch panned out, she'd save herself and Alonzo a whole lot of trouble in the morning.

The phone rang five minutes later, jarring Stephanie out of her erratic musings.

"Derek Kane—that's K-a-n-e. Thirty-two years old, owns his own landscaping business in Flowery Branch. Gave a complete statement at scene and then again at headquarters, and has requested to remain *anonymous*." There was a pause, then the voice said, "So you never heard this from me."

"Of course," Stephanie replied. "Thanks."

She ignored the little twinge of guilt she felt at having forced her friend to delve into police files.

"I only asked for verification," she reminded herself as she grabbed her suit jacket and headed to the elevator.

"And now I have it."

And now, why bother calling ahead? The element of surprise always worked best in these situations.

First thing in the morning, Stephanie intended to take a little road trip up to Lake Lanier.

To a place called Flowery Branch.

Where she hoped she'd come face-to-face with a man named Derek Kane.

Chapter Four

Derek couldn't believe it. She'd gone and told the entire story on the evening news, complete with an interview of Walter Griffin from his hospital bed. Thankfully, Walter didn't know that Derek had sat outside his room most of the night. Thankfully, the hospital staff had not divulged that someone had taken care of the man's medical bills.

So all she had was her own eyewitness account and Walter Griffin's undying gratitude for her and "the other angel" who'd saved his life, according to him.

Great. Now Derek was being billed as an angel, too.

This morning, as he stood on the deck watching the sun come up, Derek couldn't seem to find that sense of peace waking up here had always brought him. Maybe because last night he hadn't been able to find a peaceful sleep. He'd tossed and turned, reliving Stephanie Maguire's vivid account of the mugging she'd witnessed in downtown Atlanta.

Her words, spoken from a voice that was half innocent, half calculating, still remained as fresh in Derek's overworked mind as the strong brew at the bottom of his cup.

"And so, a happy ending to what could have been a tragedy. All because one man dared to step out of the shadows and help a fellow human being. Wherever that stranger, that Good Samaritan, is tonight, we thank him."

She hadn't told the world his name, at least.

Derek didn't know if that omission made him glad or mad. Women like Stephanie Maguire always had good reasons for doing the things they did. Now Derek was waiting for the other shoe to drop. Maybe it was the way she'd said it, as if she were sending out a challenge, or maybe it was the way she'd stared straight into the camera, as if she were staring straight at him, straight into his wounded heart.

"You're getting downright morose," he mumbled to himself.

Lazarus grunted, thinking that was his cue to get ready for their run.

The morning was calm and sweet with the scent of emerging wisteria and honeysuckle blossoms from the nearby woods. Out in the pines and oaks, splashes of stark white flowering trees could be seen here and there.

Dogwoods.

Derek knew the legend of the dogwood, how their blossoms represented Christ dying on the cross. Even now, from this distance he could see the white, cross-shaped flowers waving to him, comforting him. Derek needed the gentle reminder. He wasn't alone in this struggle.

Lazarus whined again, bringing Derek's attention back from the forest.

"I know, I know, Laz. I'm imagining things. I'm getting all worked up about nothing. She could have told the world my name. But she didn't."

That one act, whether intentional or out of kindness, made Derek think that maybe he was wrong about Stephanie Maguire. Maybe she wasn't like other reporters.

Too many maybes. Too much on his mind.

"Let's get going, boy." Hopping down off the deck, Derek did a few stretches, then jogged in place.

Lazarus, however, was more than ready for their run. The dog started barking and twirling in circles, anxious for his master to issue a command.

"What ails you?" Derek said, his eyes following the direction of the dog's nose. Lazarus was alert and sniffing at something.

And that's when Derek saw her.

Stephanie Maguire. In the flesh. Walking up the winding dirt drive to his lake house. She was wearing jeans, a lightweight tailored blazer and dark sunglasses.

She looked great for seven o'clock in the morning.

Lazarus apparently thought so, too. The big dog barked loudly, then turned back to Derek with beseeching eyes. Derek quickly issued a command, then watched as the dog took off running down the lane toward his lovely quarry.

Stephanie looked up just in time to see the huge dog flying toward her. She'd heard him barking, but it was too late to run now. The big animal was coming for her.

Big dog. Big teeth. Her life flashed before her eyes as she wondered why she hadn't done the sensible thing and tried calling first.

"Okay. I can handle this," she told herself as the animal galloped down the dirt lane. A German shepherd. Was he trained to kill on sight? Could she remember how to protect herself—she'd done a story on how to avoid dog bites just last year.

"Avoid eye contact," she told herself as she braced for the animal's attack. "Roll into a ball and cover your head."

Even as she went over the list of protection tips,

Stephanie knew this animal could maul her permanently with one bite.

And then she saw Derek, dressed in shorts and a T-shirt, walking casually toward her.

Surely he would call off his attack dog.

Too late, Stephanie realized he wouldn't. She could only stand there, frozen to the spot, waiting and wondering why this man would be so mean-spirited as to sic a dog on her. She didn't make eye contact with the dog, but she sure gave the man a good, long stare.

And then, because she was so distracted by the look in Derek's eyes, the big dog was on her, knocking her down to the ground before she could even manage to roll away. Gritting her teeth and closing her eyes tightly, Stephanie heard her own scream.

Her heart pounding as the animal's giant paws held her down, she waited for the sure pain of teeth sinking into her skin.

And got a wet tongue in her face instead.

"Ugh!" Opening one eye, Stephanie faced wet black-and-tan fur and another slap of wet tongue across her cheek. And a beautiful set of the darkest dog eyes she'd ever seen.

"Why, you're just a big old baby," she said, laughing from the sheer relief of not being eaten alive. Bringing a hand up, she rubbed the big animal's silky fur and heard his grunt of pleasure. "Ah, that's so sweet. So sweet. But, hey, fellow, could you let me up? This ground's cold on my backside.''

Then she heard feet crunching on the rocks. Human feet.

''Some watchdog you are,'' Derek said to the animal, his eyes on Stephanie, his expression just short of highly amused. With something next to a grunt, he told the dog to sit.

Reluctantly, the big animal did just that.

While his master stood there with his hands crossed over his chest, his whole expression a mixture of aggravation and satisfaction.

He did have the good grace to reach a hand down to her, at least. The dog moved out of the way and, after Derek gave him another command, danced around them while Derek pulled her up as if she were nothing more than a broken branch.

Stephanie accepted his hand and felt secure in that able-bodied, strong grip. In the light of day, she also became very much aware of Derek as a man. She hadn't imagined his good looks; they were very much a reality. His craggy face was a study in mystery, an interesting stony countenance that didn't invite attention. But she imagined women gave him a second look whether he liked it or not.

Annoyed by her wayward feelings, she let go, then fussed with straightening her clothes and shaking dirt out of her hair.

"Hello," she said, a lopsided smile covering her embarrassment. "Nice doggy."

Derek folded his big arms across his chest again, then gave her a long, measuring look. "A total disappointment. He always did fall for a pretty face and perfume."

Even as he said it with such sarcasm and disdain, he reached down and patted the dog on the neck, as if he were protecting the animal, a small fraction of pride measuring his wry smile.

Stephanie continued to brush twigs and dirt from her hair and clothes, then remembered she really should be mad at Derek for letting her think his dog was going to attack her. "I thought... You could have called him down, you know. He scared the daylights out of me."

"I could have," he replied, turning to head back toward the house. "But then, you could have minded your own business and stayed in the city." Tossing her a hard look over his shoulder, he asked, "So, Miss Maguire, how'd you find me, anyway?"

"I work at a television station, remember," she told him, hurrying up the sloping hill to keep pace with him. "We do research when we go after a story."

Derek whirled around then, all traces of a smile, wry or otherwise, gone from his lips. "I told you— I don't want to be a story. But since you went on the air with this anyway, I guess there's no stopping you now.''

"I didn't give out your identity."

"Gee, thanks." He started toward the deck of the house. "C'mon, Lazarus."

The dog seemed torn between obeying his master and sticking close to his new friend.

Stephanie hurried to catch up with Derek, the animal right on her heels. "Look, can't you at least talk to me, tell me why you don't want any publicity?"

"No."

"Why not?"

"Because it's none of your business."

"But people want to know. We've had so many calls and faxes and e-mails since last night. You're a hero."

Derek turned, then sank back against the deck, his whole stance hostile and unyielding. "I'm not a hero, lady. And the best thing you can do for both yourself and me is turn and walk right back down that dirt lane."

"No."

"Yes."

"Can't we just talk? Off the record."

He laughed, harsh and hard. "Yeah, right."

"I mean it," Stephanie told him. "If you tell me it's off the record, then it stays that way."

"I don't trust you."

"I know that."

"Then leave."

"I don't want to leave."

"I don't want you here. And I'm going to be late."

"Your dog—what's his name...Lazarus—*he* likes me."

"He's just a dumb animal."

Stephanie wanted to stomp her foot. He was the most stubborn man she'd ever met. And about the best-looking one, too. Just the way he stood there, all rigid and firm in his denials, made her want to get closer to him, to see what made him tick. That and the way his gray eyes changed in intensity with each passing minute. This quest could easily turn into more than a story.

"Could I have some of that great-smelling coffee?" she asked, hoping to stall the inevitable.

She watched as Derek eyed the half-empty pot sitting on the cedar picnic table. She noticed a Bible lying there, too. For some reason, that touched her, giving her confidence that this man wasn't so tough and mean after all.

Yet he looked tough, standing there, his dark, gold-streaked hair lifting in the wind, his eyes wary as he stared her down. She could almost read the expression on his face. His first instinct, naturally, was to tell her no, she couldn't have any coffee. Yet his eyes told her otherwise. That gave her hope and a kind of warm, tingling feeling in her empty stomach.

"It might still be warm," he said by way of offering her a cup. "I'll get you a mug."

"Thanks." Using another tactic, she added, "And food would be welcome. I skipped breakfast and I feel a headache coming on."

He stomped across the deck, then called over his shoulder, "Do you need an aspirin, too?"

"No. I have medicine in the car."

Derek turned his head at an angle, his hand on the knob of one of the wide glass-paneled doors. "Anything else?"

"Nothing that I can think of right now," she told him as she sank onto a comfortable deck chair, one hand buried in Lazarus's soft fur while she absently rubbed her temple with the other. After she watched Derek go inside, she whispered down to the dog, "Now, tell me all of his secrets, okay, boy?"

Lazarus gave her a doleful look, almost as if he understood her and wished he could accommodate. Then he sank down at her feet and grunted while together they waited for Derek to come back out.

Derek watched her from the huge bay window in the kitchen. She already had Lazarus wrapped around her finger. The dog was drooling and rolling around as if he'd found a patch of dry sand to wallow in.

All of Derek's instincts were screaming to send this woman away. Now. But his heart, his lonely heart, was begging him to just sit with her and share a cup of coffee. Maybe, he told himself as a means of justification, if he fed her and gave her a drink, she'd just go away and leave him alone.

Derek grabbed a heavy blue mug, saw the emblem on it, then quickly returned it to the back of the cabinet. "Don't want her to see that one." Satisfied with a white mug instead, he grabbed a box of cookies and headed back outside, his gaze following Stephanie as she dropped down on the deck to rub Lazarus's big belly.

Her laughter filled the early-morning stillness with a bright music. Derek had never heard a woman's laughter here at his private retreat. It both annoyed and enticed him.

And that made his voice edgy and harsh. "Here."

The woman at his feet looked up at him then, her big eyes as bright and open as the lake waters down by the dock. "You really don't want me here, do you?" she asked as she took the mug full of coffee.

"Nope." Derek refilled his own cup, then sank onto a deck chair, a long sigh rising out of his body.

"You look tired."

"You don't know me well enough to know what my tired look is."

"I know dark circles underneath eyes—I've certainly had my own share of those."

That comment made him wonder what she had to keep her up nights. Maybe her job. Maybe her personal life. Maybe both. No concern of his, though.

"Okay, I didn't sleep well," he told her on a snarl. "And it's your fault."

He liked the way she changed from serious reporter to confused female, all in the blink of an eye.

Then she smiled. "You were thinking about *me* last night?"

Oh, yeah. "Don't flatter yourself. I was thinking about how you seem determined to butt in to my life, even though I've asked you not to."

"I have a job to do," she replied through chews of an oatmeal cookie. She sure had an appetite.

"So that means you can just mow over people's feelings, get to the bottom of the story by stepping right on everyone's toes?"

She looked a bit guilty, then grabbed another cookie from the open box. "Wow, you really don't like reporters. Why is that?"

"Nice try, lady." Derek put his cup down with a thud. "Look, let's just cut to the chase. You are not going to get the rest of the story from me. So why don't you take your pretty little self on back to the city." He leaned forward, so that they were almost nose-to-nose, her down on the deck floor, him up in the chair. "I'm asking you nicely to let the story end right here, right now. You put together a good piece last night and now the public knows that a man was saved. That's great. But it has to end there, okay?''

He waited, watching her face, feeling his heart taking up a faster cadence. Why did she have to look so adorable, so innocent, sitting there with her hair, which still had bits of grass in it, rising out in those unruly waves.

''Why?'' she asked as she leaned closer. ''Why does it have to end?''

Derek realized then and there that this woman would not back down, nor would she be intimidated. Wondering how he could convince her that he really did not want to take this any further, he pushed closer, too. Maybe he could scare her away by implying certain things. Maybe he should flirt with her. That would probably send her running.

So he pushed. Until his face was an inch from hers, until the power of her perfume surrounded him, making him forget honeysuckle and wisteria. Until her lips parted in surprise and a questioning look crested like the sun over the lake in her luminous eyes.

''I'll tell you why, Miss Maguire,'' he said in a deliberately lazy voice. ''I have a confession to make.''

That got her attention. ''Really? Off the record?''

Derek could almost hear the mechanisms inside that beautiful head, turning and booting up like a computer drive. "Completely off the record," he replied, his voice husky and low.

"Tell me," she said, her tone just below awed.

Derek moved almost another inch, then placed a hand against her cheek. Later he would remember the tiny pulsebeat there against her slender neck. Later he would remember a lot of things and wonder what had come over him. But right now he believed he was doing the only thing he could to get rid of her.

"I...I have a thing for you, Miss Maguire." He chuckled as he pulled a twig of pine straw from her hair. "I reckon half the men in Atlanta have a crush on you, though. But...I got lucky—I mean, you're here with me. You actually want to get to know me better, right?"

"I want to hear your story, yes."

He saw the doubt flaring up in her eyes, and felt a sudden surge of victory. Thinking he'd found her weak spot, Derek plunged right ahead. "But why stop there? Why not take it a step further? Why not let *me* get to know *you,* too? We could have dinner, share a few laughs. What do you say? I'd love to be able to tell my friends I dated the famous Stephanie Maguire."

He watched her swallow, watched her eyes grow even wider, watched her long lashes flutter like butterfly wings against the satin skin of her cheekbones. If there was a shard of disappointment there in the blues and greens of her eyes, he told himself he didn't care. He had to convince her to leave him alone. The disappointment passed like a cloud over water, then he saw her struggling—did she take him up on his offer and use that as an excuse to get her story, or did she jump up and run away as fast as her long legs could carry her?

Deciding to help her along, Derek put his other hand on her other cheek, then urged her face to his. A kiss to seal the deal. And get her off his back forever.

But when his lips touched hers, when his lips felt the softness, the open welcome of her spice-scented warmth, Derek realized too late that his plan had somehow backfired. Stephanie Maguire kissed him back. And he liked it.

Lifting his head, he glared down into her face, his eyes meeting hers as he pulled away. Frustrated beyond repair, he had to finish the charade. In a shaky voice he asked, "So, what do you think?"

As if she were coming out of a trance, Stephanie lifted herself up off the deck, then put as much distance between herself and him as she could. "I think it's time for me to leave."

Happy that her voice sounded as creaky and shaky as his own, Derek regained some of his earlier spunk. "What, now? I thought you wanted to talk to me?"

She held up a hand. "Talk, yes. I don't recall

anything about kissing you, however. This is strictly business, I assure you, Mr. Kane.''

''Ah, I hate to hear that,'' he said, dancing a jig in his mind. ''I guess I just got carried away, what with you being you and all. I do apologize.''

''It's...it's all right. I understand. I hope I didn't give you the wrong impression. And I have to go.''

She backed down the steps, almost tripping in her haste to get on down the road. Lazarus, confused by this new game, whined and pawed the dirt, hoping to bring back his friend.

But she was halfway down the lane. Derek watched her round the curve. She sure was a fast walker.

As he heard the roar of a car engine down on the road, he had to grin. It had worked. Derek Kane had found the chink in the great armor of hotshot reporter Stephanie Maguire. She wanted every story but her own revealed.

And after that kiss, he wanted to know everything there was to know about her.

Too bad he'd never have that chance.

Chapter Five

❧

"This will be a good chance to mingle with some of our most influential viewers, Stef. You have to go." Claire Cook scrunched up her pert nose and stared down at Stephanie through her black bifocals. "You get to dress up."

"I don't want to dress up and I don't want to go," Stephanie told her, one hand on her computer save button and the other already reaching for the phone. "I'm busy."

"The invitation requested you and you alone," Claire reminded her. "They want you there to lend support to their cause."

Stephanie dropped the phone and whirled in her swivel chair to stare up at her boss. "I do support the annual Azalea Pilgrimage. You know I send them a check each year. But that doesn't mean I have to make nice with a bunch of rich people at a reception.''

''Yes, it does,'' Claire replied, her nose still scrunched. ''You will go and you will enjoy.''

''Is that an order?''

Claire nodded, causing her orange loop earrings to move in slow motion against her freckled neck. ''In the nicest possible way.''

Stephanie sighed long and hard. Since she really didn't have a social life, this would be a good chance to get out and meet people. And she just might find a story in that elite crowd. Maybe ask the mayor about his tough stance on crime, maybe pin down a congressman or senator regarding the current legislative session.

Lifting her hands through her hair, she bobbed her head. ''Okay, all right. I'll go. When is it? Next week?''

Claire beamed. ''Tomorrow night.''

Stephanie groaned. ''Tomorrow? But I've got so much to do—''

Claire raised a hand to interrupt her. ''I put the invitation on your desk over a week ago, hoping to hear a response. It's at Nadine Hamilton's home.''

Stephanie lifted a brow, then snatched the gold-embossed card from Claire's hand so she could scan the elaborately printed words. ''*The* Nadine Hamilton?''

''The only one,'' Claire replied with a smug

smile. "That would be the Nadine Hamilton who has enough money to buy out Ted Turner if she set her mind to it. Well, maybe not that much. But we both know the woman is rich…and very generous with her money, too."

Stephanie had to agree there. Nadine Hamilton was one of the most prominent citizens of Atlanta, having come from stock that had helped build the city. A staunch Christian, she was always receiving plaques and awards for her philanthropist work. Everyone in Atlanta admired the woman, and most of the cream of Atlanta society was scared to do anything to offend her.

"It would be rude to say no to Miss Nadine," Stephanie said, sorry that she'd whined so much about being invited to the kickoff reception for the annual Azalea Pilgrimage, which was being held at Miss Nadine's spacious mansion.

Claire tapped the invitation. "Rude, and in our case, to decline or not show up would put a bad light on the entire television station. I'm counting on your charm and good manners to win the day, however."

"Oh, sure." Stephanie thought about all the work she had to do—two stories to edit for airings later in the week, and…more pondering about Derek Kane. But she knew how persistent Claire could be when she wanted something. "It's just for a couple of hours, right? I guess I can manage that. And I'll snag some interviews while I'm there, then come back here and work late—again.''

"Now you're talking," Claire said, clearly relieved. "You can take a camera crew, cover the event. We'll run it at the end of tomorrow night's newscast, just to please Miss Nadine and her powerful friends. I'm glad you're going.''

"Who's going where?"

Both Stephanie and Claire turned to find James Glover standing there, listening to their conversation.

Claire rolled her eyes. "James, don't you have somebody else to annoy?"

"Now, is that any way to talk to your…number-two reporter?" James, curly haired and stocky, with a charming smile, shot Stephanie a good-natured glare. "What's up with you two?"

Knowing he'd badger her until she told him, Stephanie said, "I'm going to cover Miss Nadine's reception for the Azalea Pilgrimage tomorrow night. Want to tag along?"

James looked interested, then turned to Claire. "What do you say, boss?"

Claire studied Stephanie as if to say, "Are you sure?" then nodded. "Yeah, why not? James, you can be Stephanie's escort. Between the two of you, I expect some good PR for Miss Nadine and some good solid leads for future stories, if you get my drift."

"I get your drift," James said, his brown eyes glistening with delight. "A lot of important people will be there. I'll keep my ears to the ground."

"That's my boy," Claire said, waving goodbye to them.

"You don't mind being my date?" James asked after Claire had left.

"It's not a date, Glover," Stephanie reminded him. "It's work."

"Oh, right. We agreed to keep things strictly business between us. Hey, no problem."

Stephanie had to grin. James was sweet and lovable, but not her type. They'd established the ground rules long ago, when he'd first come to the station from a smaller network in Alabama. But he still liked to tease her. And he also liked to stay on her heels, trying to surpass her as the number-one reporter at WNT. So far, he hadn't been able to overcome her solid ratings. But it was a friendly competition, at least on Stephanie's part. Sometimes, however, she wondered if James didn't resent her just a bit. He certainly liked to taunt her and he surely seemed too ambitious at times. But maybe that was just his nature.

"So, around five o'clock?" she said now, thinking she had to get back to work herself. "We could change here and go there straight from work."

James nodded. "I'll be ready."

"And Glover," she called as he walked away, "black tie optional."

"I'll dress the part," he told her with a passing wave.

That made her stop and think what she should wear to the fancy event. Looking down, she realized she still had on the jacket and jeans she'd hurriedly donned before daylight, just so she could get out to Derek Kane's house before work.

"And you sure got that story nailed down," she told herself, a hot flush rising up her neck in spite of her ability to always look calm and in control.

He'd kissed her!

And now, belatedly, she understood exactly why he'd done it. He'd wanted to get rid of her. Fast.

"Well, it worked, Mr. Kane," she said on a low whisper as she scanned her computer screen. "But not for long. I'm not so easily swayed. I'll be back and I'll find out what you're hiding."

If Derek Kane thought a mere kiss would scare off Stephanie Maguire, he was wrong. Very wrong.

He didn't need to know that kiss had made her stop and ponder more than once. In fact, thoughts of Derek had disrupted her work all day long. The kiss hadn't caused her to back off, however. On the contrary, it had only made her want to get to know him even better.

And she would find a way to do that. Soon.

Just as soon as she figured out how to win over

a man who obviously didn't trust reporters. A man who'd been desperate enough to kiss her just to get rid of her.

"If you don't trust reporters, that means you've had dealings with them in the past. So…"

She'd keep looking, keep searching, until she found out what was up with Derek Kane.

And in the meantime, she'd put that kiss right out of her head. She touched a hand to her lips even as she pledged to do just that.

Derek had to whistle at the sheer magnificence of the place. Miss Nadine has surely pulled out all the stops for this night. Including sending her own personal car to pick him up, with a driver who'd handed him a tuxedo and an engraved invitation that read: "Mr. Kane, please put on this tuxedo and come and share in the opening reception of the annual Atlanta Azalea Pilgrimage. I insist."

Which meant, in Miss Nadine speak, you'd better be here and on time, buddy.

She invited him every year, and every year Derek came up with some feeble excuse. He did not fit in with rich people and old money. Not one bit.

So why was he here tonight, standing on the terrace of Nadine Hamilton's lavish mansion, watching the crowd of beautiful people who insisted on trampling over the grass he'd so lovingly cultivated for this very event?

Maybe because this year he needed the distraction. He needed the affirmation that his work had paid off, that his back ached because he'd put in a good day's work and that this garden was beautiful, precious and priceless because he'd taken the time to nurture it. Maybe he just wanted to put Stephanie Maguire out of his mind.

So far, it wasn't working. He'd tried for a whole two days. He'd worked hard, exercised hard, played hard, prayed hard, but to no avail. She was there in his dreams each night. And each morning the memory of her laughter echoed out over his once tranquil backyard. He'd even tried watching another newscast, but somehow the remote control always brought him back to her face, her smile, her lips.

So now, to escape, he'd given in and put on a tuxedo to come here amid the beautiful people, hoping the sight of this garden he loved so much would bring him some comfort.

He felt completely lost and out of place.

So he just stood there, listening to the interesting conversation, listening to the night sounds, watching as a white-gold sunset filtered through the rich green leaves of a century-old magnolia tree. Down below, the sun's soft rays shot out to form a rainbow of color above the tinkling fountain that sprayed down into Miss Nadine's prized rock-formed waterfall.

''Beautiful, isn't it?'' Miss Nadine asked as she

came to stand next to Derek. "I'm so glad you finally came, Mr. Kane."

Derek nodded his respect. "I guess I never felt worthy of coming here before. I mean, once my work was done and everything."

"Nonsense," Miss Nadine replied, reaching up to adjust his black bow tie. "This is your garden, your masterpiece. You deserve to share in the credit."

"No," Derek corrected, "this is God's masterpiece. I just took what He offered and worked with it."

"Well, you both did a tremendous job," the old woman replied. "And I'm thankful."

Derek smiled down at her. "You look sharp tonight, Miss Nadine."

She preened, whirling in her teal watered silk formal gown. "I'm content with my lot in life." Then she urged him down the steps. "But you, young man, need to go and meet some of these people. Might garner a few more clients. You've taken enough of my money. Go pick on somebody else."

"I just might, at that," Derek said, his hand on Miss Nadine's arm, his gaze sweeping the garden.

And then he saw *her*.

Miss Nadine must have felt him stiffen. The old woman glanced up at him, then looked out to where Derek was staring. "She's lovely, isn't she?"

Derek didn't speak. He couldn't.

Stephanie Maguire was standing in the middle of

the garden, *his* garden, and she rivaled any flowers blooming here tonight. She was dressed in white— white except for a cascading sprig of embroidered blue flowers that moved down the skirt of her flowing gown, almost as if someone had tossed them there and they'd fallen across the wispy material at random. Her dark hair was up in a curled arrangement that left little wisps falling around her face and neck. And around her shoulders, covering the wide straps of her gown, she wore a gauzy matching white wrap that boasted one lost blue blossom across its flowing end.

She took his breath away.

Miss Nadine gave Derek a friendly poke in the ribs. "Well, don't just stand there. Go and meet Miss Maguire. Or shall I introduce you?"

"We've met," Derek managed to say. Then, because the older woman was pinning a questioning glance or him with her all-seeing eyes, he added, "I'll go down and say hello."

"Well, see that you do. She's here to spread the word about the pilgrimage. You might mention that you were in charge of getting the gardens in order for the entire event."

"I might," he replied, his eyes still fixed on the woman across the garden.

Then again, he might just turn around and leave by the back way, since he didn't want to give Stephanie any more personal information to fuel her fire.

He was just about to do that very thing when Stephanie looked up and right into his eyes.

Surprise. She was surprised to see him here. That figured. Then a shy smile. She was smiling at him. That didn't figure. She was supposed to be mad at him.

"Of all the gardens…"

Derek realized mumbling to himself wouldn't help him out of this spot. Should he pray that Stephanie Maguire didn't find out about his involvement with this project? Oh, she'd just love to broadcast that bit of information to the world, wouldn't she?

Lord, I've been in tighter spots. And You've helped me out of those. Show me what to do next. Help me.

And then Stephanie started walking toward him, and Derek became helplessly, completely lost all over again.

She couldn't believe it was really him. Stephanie had to take a deep, calming breath or she would certainly make a fool of herself. She'd been waiting none too patiently for Glover to bring her a goblet of Miss Nadine's famous lemon, vanilla and mint iced tea, when she'd glanced up to find Derek Kane, wearing a tuxedo, standing on the terrace. At first she honestly believed she'd somehow imagined him there.

But the man making his way down the steps was

very real. And even more intriguing than ever before. What was he doing here, at one of the social events of the year? Was he rich—the millionaire-next-door type who didn't like to flaunt his wealth? That would explain why he didn't want any publicity. Or maybe since he was a landscaper, he'd come here to inspect the breathtaking gardens, scope out the competition. That would certainly make sense.

Then another thought emerged in her starstruck mind. What if Derek were here with someone? After all, she'd never even asked if he was attached. His records had stated that he was single, but...

She didn't see any of the elegantly dressed females in the crowd coming forward to claim him, although several of them cut their eyes toward him as he made his way through the sloping gardens.

Stephanie couldn't help but be relieved. She didn't think she could stand here and be polite if another woman was draped on Derek's arm. Then she immediately pushed such thoughts right out of her head. *He means nothing to you, besides a story. Remember that. And his kiss can't mean anything. It was a trick. Remember that, too.*

But as Derek finally reached her, Stephanie's only memories were centered around his bewildered, lopsided smile and the feel of his lips pressed against hers the last time they'd been together.

Those memories must have shown in her face.

"Hello," he said, taking her arm to guide her to

a quiet corner of the yard. "You look positively dreamy."

She tried to laugh, but it came out as a breathless giggle. "Dreamy? That's a new one."

"Okay, how about you look like a dream?"

"Thank you." She nodded her head, causing a wayward curl to fall over her brow. "You look pretty terrific yourself." Glancing at his feet, she added, "What, no cowboy boots tonight?"

He shrugged. "Miss Nadine picked out my outfit. It didn't include boots."

Stephanie's mind started whirling. "So, you and Miss Nadine are good friends, then?"

He shrugged, glanced around at the crowd. "The best."

He wasn't going to make this easy, she realized. But then, he never had. "How'd you come to know her?"

"Gardening."

Stephanie pushed at her hair, then counted two beats to set the pace. She had to play it cool, or he'd realize she was interrogating him. "Oh, you mean through your landscaping business?" At his surprised look, she added, "I've learned that much about you, at least."

He glanced around, then back at Stephanie, and took his dear sweet time answering. "I've helped her out with the pilgrimage for a few years now. Just tips here and there."

"So you both serve in some of the same organizations, charity drives, functions?"

"You might say that."

Tossing her sheer wrap across her shoulder, Stephanie gave him a frustrated look. "You certainly are a man of few words."

"Yep. And you certainly ask too many questions."

"It's my nature."

From the gazebo, an ensemble of musicians struck up a rendition of "Waltz of the Flowers" from the *Nutcracker.* Cellos and violins softly played Tchaikovsky as people chatted and laughed.

Stephanie was wondering what to say next when Derek took her hand in his. "I don't talk, but I do dance. Would you like to—dance that is?"

"Well, you are full of surprises," she said as she indicated yes with a lowering of her head.

Instead of taking her into a waltz, he pulled her forward. "Not here. I know another place, more private."

Stephanie's heart reached a crescendo, then swayed right along with the music. Derek Kane wanted to dance with her, in private.

Coming to her senses, she yanked her hand back. "Wait. Is this another ploy to distract me, to scare me away, like that kiss the other day?"

He turned to stare down into her eyes. "*Did* that kiss the other day distract you?"

She gave him her best professional glare. "Not for long."

"Well, did it scare you away?"

"Not for long," she repeated, staring back up at him measure for measure, waiting for both a denial and an explanation.

Derek didn't give her either. Instead, he took her hand again and half dragged her down the sloping hills, deep into the maze of hundreds of dusk-kissed fuchsia- and violet-tinged azalea blossoms and towering, white-blooming magnolia trees. He didn't speak or stop until they'd reached another gazebo, this one smaller and made of sweet-smelling, rich brown cedar.

Then after he'd tugged her inside the screen of the lattice-covered, octagon-shaped walls, he pulled her into his arms and said, "You should be scared. In fact, if you're smart, you'll turn and run away from me right now, before I do something really crazy, like kiss you again."

Chapter Six

"You wouldn't dare kiss me again," Stephanie said as she backed out of his embrace. "It won't work again, Derek. You can't get to me."

He stepped closer. "Oh, yeah? Well, you sure seemed to be in a big hurry the other morning."

"I had to get to work."

"Yeah, right."

Appalled that he actually *knew* how he'd affected her, she said, "Believe it or not, I do have other stories to work on, other people to interview. You and your story aren't that high up on my list anymore."

"Good. Then my work is done."

He turned to leave, but she caught him by the arm. "Oh, no, you don't. You can't just bring me out here, threaten to kiss me, warn me away from you, then just leave me standing here.''

"And why can't I? You just made it clear you no longer want me around. Which is fine by me, by the way.''

Stephanie let loose a long sigh, causing her wayward bangs to fan out over her brow. "I didn't say I didn't want you around. I'd really like us to talk, Derek. Really talk. Like two polite adults.''

"For your story?''

"No, for myself,'' she admitted, dropping her gaze down to the planked floor. "I...I just don't want to fight with you anymore.''

Something in her tone touched a chord in Derek's heart. Maybe it was the way she refused to look at him, the way she had her head down, her lips in an almost believable pout.

He lifted her chin with the pad of his thumb, then reached up to brush her irresistible hair out of her eyes. "I don't want to fight anymore either, Stephanie.''

"Truce?''

He could see the sincerity in the depths of her eyes. And he could also see something else there— a vulnerability that tore at his heartstrings. Maybe he'd been too harsh, too unfair to this woman. "Truce,'' he said. Then, "Now what about that dance?''

"Are you sure?''

"Yeah, but I'd better warn you about something else, too."

"Oh, and what's that?"

"I can't really dance."

That brought a smile to her lips. "How about I lead, then?"

"Now there's a scary thought." He took her into his arms, determined to make an attempt. "I can do the boot-scooting-boogie, but not this fancy stuff."

She laughed again. "You know, it doesn't really matter. We're alone and I won't showcase your lack of dancing skills on the eleven-o'clock news."

"Promise?"

"Promise. I won't even mention that I saw you here."

That brought him some measure of relief. "I think we've reached an understanding of sorts, Miss Maguire." But before he could be sure, he had another question. "Why *didn't* you reveal my name when you did the story about the mugging?"

"You asked me not to."

Impressed but still cynical, he said, "You don't strike me as the type to back down, though. I figured you'd just go right ahead and tell half the state of Georgia, regardless of how I felt."

She dropped her head again, then lifted her gaze to him. "Derek, I'm not such a horrible person. Just like you, I'm a Christian—although not a perfect one—and I do honor people's requests. I'd only go against that if withholding information could hurt someone or hinder an investigation."

He gave her a wry grin. "So I'm really, truly not being investigated anymore?"

She shrugged, causing her wrap to fall away from her arms. "The story's old news now. In spite of the intense interest, people will forget. What's the point?"

"But you're still curious?"

"Of course. I'm a reporter. And I do have a vested interest, since I was also involved. Right now I'm waiting to hear the outcome of the court case." She paused, then stared into his eyes. "But...things have changed. Now I'd just like to get to know *you*."

He thought he'd like that, too—to get to know her. But he had to be sure of her motives. And he had a few questions of his own.

"How do you know I'm a Christian?" he asked, curious as to how she'd figured that out.

"Like I said, I'm a reporter. I'm very observant. I saw a Bible lying on your picnic table."

And what else had she observed? he wondered.

"What if that was just for show?"

"I don't believe that. Since you weren't expecting any visitors, I think that Bible was there because you wanted it there, because you read it."

He shifted his head, giving her a sideways glance.

"So, now that you think I'm a good Bible-toting person, you feel better about things?"

"Yes. My mother is always telling me to date fellow Christians. But I knew you were a good person the night I met you, even though you *were* rather rude to me."

He smiled then. "Sorry. Force of habit. I just...I like my privacy."

"I can respect that."

Derek hoped she meant that. He wanted to know her, be with her more. But he wasn't so sure he could take that chance. Still, she was standing here, being completely up front with him, something he couldn't do with her. Not now. Maybe not ever.

But he had tonight.

"Let's forget all this and pretend we're just two people who like each other and want to share a dance, okay?"

"Okay."

She allowed him to take her back into his arms. Slowly, with measured precision, they waltzed around the small enclosure of the gazebo as dusk turned to night around them and the perfume of magnolias, honeysuckle and azaleas filled their senses with an enticing richness.

The music ended, but Derek held her there, refusing to let her go. "That was nice. Maybe we should just not talk so much."

She held her hands on his chest. "And maybe I should stop prying so much."

"Will you?"

"I did promise to try."

Derek adjusted her wrap back across her arms. "I'd like that."

"Okay."

"Maybe we could even become friends...of a sort."

She repeated his phrase. "I'd like that."

"Okay."

Derek hugged her close again, relieved that he'd somehow managed to turn her from enemy to friend, but worried, too—worried that they'd just crossed another threshold. One that could be much more dangerous and revealing than any story she might ever write about him.

And yet, he couldn't let her go. Not now. Maybe not ever.

A while later, they made their way back to the crowd, a comfortable bond now developing between them. Stephanie hoped she could keep her promise. The curiosity of wanting to tell Derek's story to the world battled with the need to find out more about him on a personal level. If she went against the promise she'd made, it would destroy any chances she might have of being with Derek.

Stopping, she had to wonder when this had

changed from a news story to a budding relationship. Was she ready to take that next step? She'd asked God so many times to send her a hero, a good man who'd measure up to her father's impeccable reputation, someone she could love and cherish the way her mother had loved her father.

Is this that man, Lord?

Derek must have sensed her withdrawal. Turning, he said, "Hey, what's the matter?"

"Oh, nothing. Just thinking. I still really don't know anything about you." Stephanie glanced around, then whispered, "Except that you're a landscaper, you have a Bible and a dog named Lazarus, and...you're a hero—whether you want to be or not."

"That's all you need to know," he said, his voice low and gravelly. "And I told you, I'm not a hero. I just did what I had to do."

"Maybe." She watched his expression darkening. He didn't like talking about himself at all. And she had promised to quit prying. "Still, I would like to hear your story," she said, hoping he would understand what she was trying to tell him.

Misunderstanding, he said, "I thought you'd *dropped* the story."

"I have. That doesn't mean I have to forget I ever met you, does it?"

"Stephanie?"

She turned to find Glover barreling down on

them, two watery glasses of tea in his hand. "Oh, James. I forgot about you. I'm sorry."

Looking winded and aggravated, James Glover gave Derek the once-over, then turned to Stephanie. "Did you forget that we're here to cover this event, too? I've been interviewing people left and right. What have you been up to?"

Stephanie couldn't tell him who Derek was, so she did the next best thing. "I've been discussing…things with…my new friend here. He helped Miss Nadine get the gardens ready for the pilgrimage."

With an interested expression, James Glover shoved a mint tea into Stephanie's hand and reached across to shake Derek's hand. "Hello, I'm James Glover, Stephanie's colleague at WNT. Are you the one Miss Nadine kept insisting I interview? The master gardener, landscaping genius—she went on and on about you. Said you did all of this almost single-handedly." Before Derek could respond, Glover was motioning for the cameraman who hovered a few feet away, getting a wide shot of the crowd.

Stephanie glanced over at Derek. "I thought you just gave her a few tips here and there."

Derek shot her a warning look, but managed to shrug it away before he spotted the approaching cameraman. "Miss Nadine tends to exaggerate. I just helped her put in some flower beds."

James rolled his eyes and held up a hand. "Stephanie, have you lost your touch? You're talking to the man himself. According to Miss Hamilton, Derek Kane is one of the best gardeners in Atlanta—he was in charge of getting all of the gardens on the tour ready." Nodding toward Derek, he added, "And I understand you own your own landscaping and nursery business?"

Stephanie gulped in a deep breath. Glover knew Derek's name now—apparently Miss Nadine had told him. It wouldn't do for the sharp-nosed reporter to put two and two together and realize that this was the same man who'd been dubbed the Good Samaritan just days ago. Glover would take the story and run with it, trying to win points with both Claire and Nadine Hamilton.

And if anybody told Derek's story, it would be her.

Ambition warring with the promise she'd just made to Derek, she said a quick prayer for guidance and turned to James. "Let's go interview Miss Nadine again. And what about Senator Ruston—didn't I see him with his wife over there by the crape myrtle?"

James looked confused. "I want to talk to your friend here right now, Stef. You go talk to the senator. He likes you better, anyway."

Stephanie shot Derek a beseeching look, then held

up a hand to warn away the confused cameraman. "Not right now, James."

"I'm sorry," Derek said to James, his back now to the camera. "I was just leaving, anyway. I really need to get home."

James looked defeated, but as alert as a bulldog. "Oh. Are you sure? It would only take a couple of minutes."

"I really don't have time," Derek said. Then turning to Stephanie, he added, "If you'll excuse me, Stephanie."

"Of course." Helplessly, Stephanie watched as he made his way through the crowded garden to the inside of the house.

And then he was gone. Again.

"What was that all about?" James asked, his eyes wide.

Stephanie took a long swallow of the spicy tea. "What?"

James wagged a finger at her face. "I know you, Stephanie. It's not like you to pass on an interview, even a lightweight one with a gardener during a spring fling. You practically threw yourself between that man and the camera. What's the deal?"

"No deal," Stephanie said, whirling to walk away. She didn't like being dishonest with James, but she had to protect Derek's privacy. "Let's just find the senator and get this job done. I think I'm getting a headache."

James was right on her heels. "Okay, all right, you don't have to fake a migraine."

That set her to the boiling point. "I don't fake my migraines, James. They are very real, and if you don't get out of my face, I'm going to get a real doozy. And I don't want to miss work tomorrow."

He held up a hand, palm out. "I'm sorry. That was a low blow. I've seen you with a headache and it's not something you'd tease about. But something is up. And you know I'll just pester you until you tell me what it is."

"Yes, I know," Stephanie replied, her gaze scanning the crowd for one last glimpse of Derek. "And that's what scares me," she said under her breath.

The next morning at work, Stephanie was going over some reports with Claire when James walked up. The initial hearing for the two juveniles was set for today, and she wanted to be there.

"Did you tell Claire about our fun time at Miss Nadine's reception?" he asked before shoving a chocolate doughnut into his mouth.

"She saw the piece," Stephanie replied, her mind on her workload. "The reception was nice, though. The gardens were breathtaking, and we got some good comments from the mayor and several other prominent citizens."

Glover chewed, then said, "Yeah, but Stef here

passed up the chance to get an exclusive with the man behind all that springtime loveliness.''

Claire glanced up then, straining her neck to stare at Stephanie. ''Well, I know it wasn't a train wreck or a corrupt politician, but that would have added a nice touch. What gives?''

Stephanie shot James a hard glare. ''He had to leave the party. I couldn't very well chase him down in the front yard.''

''And why not?'' Claire asked, her eyes widening.

''It wasn't that big of a story,'' Stephanie tried to explain. ''He said he just gave her a few tips.''

James shook his head, causing his curly hair to bob around his forehead. ''No, that's where you're wrong. Derek Kane was behind the whole layout of Miss Nadine's garden. The man designed and cultivated her entire acreage and several of the gardens of some of the most prominent families in Atlanta. He would have been a good source of information and it would have given us several angles on spring gardening.''

''Did you say Derek Kane?'' Claire asked, her gaze shifting from James's florid face to Stephanie. ''Would that be the same Derek Kane—''

''That had to leave the party early,'' Stephanie interrupted, giving Claire a kick underneath the desk. ''As I said, the man didn't have time for an on-the-spot interview and so I let him go. Besides, it was a short piece on a lightweight subject. We got plenty of footage and we talked to Nadine Hamilton and the mayor of Atlanta, so what's the problem? We did our job.''

Claire took the hint. Giving James an eloquent shrug, she said, ''Don't sweat it, Jamie. Now go on and get out of here. Find some big fish to fry or something.''

James finished his doughnut, then greedily licked his fingers. ''Well, I don't get it. I think Stef here's holding out on me. Are you going to do an exclusive, in-depth story on this man? You did go off in the dark with him. Did you get some juicy secrets on mulch and watering cycles?''

''Leave now,'' Claire told James, her tone no-nonsense.

''Sorry.'' With a toss of his napkin into the trash, James bowed and headed back up the wide aisle to his own cubicle.

When he was well out of earshot, Claire grabbed Stephanie's arm, pressing her glossy orange fingernails into Stephanie's bare skin. ''You saw Derek Kane at the reception?''

''Yes,'' Stephanie whispered, afraid James would be lurking behind the cubicle wall. ''And I promised not to reveal his identity—again.''

''But…that would have been the perfect opportunity to highlight his heroic nature,'' Claire said, a hand moving through her spiky hair. ''I mean, I can understand passing on the gardener connection— that's warm and fuzzy and fluffy—but here stands the very man you've been trying to snag an exclusive interview with, the man everyone in Atlanta is calling a Good Samaritan, and you just let him walk away. What's up with that, Stef?''

''Nothing,'' Stephanie said, tossing a file across her desk with nonchalant ease. ''I just didn't want to put him on the spot.''

Claire reached a freckled hand across to place on Stephanie's forehead, her gaze scanning Stephanie's face. ''No, no signs of fever. Let me check your eyes. No, they don't look red. Can't blame it on the flu.'' Dropping her hand, she eyed Stephanie closely. ''Putting people on the spot is part of your job, honey.''

Stephanie ducked her head, hoping Claire wouldn't see the truth in her eyes.

Too late. Claire reached out again to lift Stephanie's chin with a firm hand. ''Oh, my. Oh, my my my. You…you actually have feelings for our hero, don't you?''

''No,'' Stephanie immediately denied. Then ''Yes, well, maybe. I don't know.''

''Well, I certainly do,'' Claire said, getting up to stand over her. ''That's the only explanation for this sudden show of good conscience, this change of heart. You're falling for Derek Kane, aren't you, Stephanie?''

Chapter Seven

That afternoon, Stephanie went to the hearing set for the two juveniles who'd mugged Walter Griffin. Hoping Derek would be there, she wasn't surprised when he didn't show up. They had his statement, but she wondered how he'd managed to get out of appearing at the court hearing. While neither of them had had to appear for the initial intake hearing, this one was being held before a juvenile court judge, which meant she and Derek might be called to testify. She was beginning to think he had a connection with the police department.

And she sure wondered if she'd ever see him or hear from him again. James hadn't helped the situation by insisting that they interview Derek at the garden party. Now she'd have to start all over again to win Derek's trust. And she'd been so close last night. She'd always cherish that special time she'd shared with Derek in the cedar gazebo of Miss Nadine's beautiful garden, a garden into which Derek had apparently put a lot of love and nurturing. He was that kind of man. She didn't need to dig any deeper to see that.

Sitting in the courtroom, reliving the event that had brought Derek and her together, only made her more curious about him. But since she was supposed to be covering this for a follow-up story, she had to listen to the details of the case. If the judge decided to take things further, she would have to give her own eyewitness account of the crime.

Soon, however, it was all over. The district attorney settled for a plea bargain, meaning no one would have to testify after all, then the judge put the two juveniles on probation with the stipulation that they both do extensive community service in a scheduled and carefully monitored work program to make up for their crime. The stern judge, who was known for doing everything in his power to save young people from a life of crime, informed the two that he'd set up their work schedule with their probation officer.

"And I think you'll both learn a valuable lesson from the assignment I'm giving you over the summer," the judge said in an almost gleeful tone.

That got Stephanie wondering what exactly the teens would be expected to do. But because of the nature of the plea bargain, the judge wasn't divulging that information. Which probably meant the two had given out information on someone with a much worse criminal record than their own, and would be working under protected custody. She'd have to do some digging on her own, she supposed.

All in all, the hearing was routine and over in about thirty minutes, with the two offenders glaring and trying not to look scared.

"They're only boys, Lord," she said as she left the courtroom. One black, tall and lean, the other white, more rounded and husky. What would possess them to do something so violent? She certainly hoped the judge had done the right thing by keeping them out of juvenile detention. Maybe a summer of hard work would turn them around. She sent up a prayer for that hope.

Later, back at her desk at work, Stephanie once again thought of Derek. Memories of their time together in Miss Nadine's garden brightened her work day. He'd been so...so wonderful. Sweet, understanding, gentle. She'd wanted so much to sit in that gazebo all night and talk to him. She really enjoyed his company.

But now he would probably never call her again. Now she had the added worry of keeping James Glover off the case. He'd been sniffing around all day, asking questions, prying more than she ever had. What if he found out about Derek being the Good Samaritan?

James would take the story and run with it.

Unless she beat him to it, of course.

That put an idea into her head. Maybe she could just go ahead and investigate further, on the side, in a quiet way, so as not to attract any attention. Then she'd piece things together and have it all figured out, just in case James did stumble on the truth. That way, Claire would have to give Stephanie the exclusive, since the original story had been hers anyway.

It was the only plan she could come up with in order to protect Derek's privacy and guard her story. She didn't want this in James Glover's hot little hands. Not at all.

And if Derek found out she'd gone against her promise, she'd just have to make him understand she was doing this to help him, to keep him safely out of the limelight, just as he'd requested. She'd have to keep James off the trail until the story was old news, but if he did find out, Stephanie would have the option to bury the story.

"Are you burying another bone?" Derek called to Lazarus as they walked the lake's rounded shoreline. "At least you refrain from digging and burying while we're at Miss Nadine's, you ol' lazy thing."

The dog was up ahead, grunting, a clean steak

bone caught between his teeth. He answered his master by slinging dirt and wagging his tail.

"Well, don't let me interrupt," Derek said, more to himself than the big animal. "While you bury that bone, maybe I should bury the hatchet and call Stephanie."

Derek decided he had some unfinished business with the lovely reporter. Still amazed at having seen her there in the garden, he wanted to see her here in his own garden again. He wanted to talk to her, learn all her secrets, feed her homemade ice cream, take her for a boat ride on the lake. They had been interrupted way too soon the other night and he wanted to take up where they'd left off.

"But that was with yet another reporter nipping at your heels," he reminded himself. And one not nearly as attractive as Stephanie Maguire.

If he called her, they could at least talk.

If he called her, it could open up a whole new world of hurts.

What if that other guy didn't give up the way Stephanie had? And why had she given up so easily? Was she doing the honorable thing, or was she up to something else entirely? What if that other guy, Glover, *didn't* always do the honorable thing? Maybe Glover and Stephanie were in on this together somehow.

It was enough to drive a man to distraction. Which is exactly what Stephanie Maguire had done since the night he'd met her. Maybe even before then.

Derek knew he'd be taking a chance on developing a relationship with Stephanie Maguire. Especially now, when he'd just agreed to take on what might turn out to be his most challenging project. Yet it was a chance he was more than willing to take.

He looked out over the clear, still waters and asked God to guide him. "What should I do, Lord?"

He stood there, listening, waiting, letting the peaceful, lapping waters soothe him, letting the smell of evergreen and pine assault his senses. Across the way, a pair of wood ducks clucked and fussed, their babies trailing behind them on the gentle water.

Lazarus finished his task, barked halfheartedly at his duck friends for good measure, then came bounding up. Derek clapped at the dog, letting Lazarus jump up, two dirty paws splattering mud and dirt across Derek's worn jeans. "What do you think, boy?"

Lazarus whined and drooled.

"We're in the same boat," Derek said, pushing the heavy dog away. "C'mon, Laz. We've got a phone call to make."

Two days later Stephanie pulled her tiny green sports car up the winding drive to Derek's lakeside retreat, her nerves in tangles, her mind whirling with mixed emotions.

She'd been digging into Derek's past, but so far she hadn't come up with much besides the basic stats—except the surprising information that she'd received from Walter Griffin.

Thinking that maybe the old man might remember something else from the night he was mugged, some detail from his brief conversation with Derek, she'd gone to find Walter at the downtown homeless shelter where he sometimes stayed, according to the address he'd given the police. She'd also wanted to talk to Walter regarding her follow-up story and get his reaction to the judge sentencing his attackers to community service.

Walter was doing better, in spite of the lingering bruises covering his face. He looked gaunt and shaky, but his eyes were clear and bright.

"Miss Maguire," he said in his raspy, breathless voice. "It's good to see you again."

"How are you, Mr. Griffin?"

Walter waved a hand for her to sit down on the vinyl couch in the rec room where he'd been watching an old Western on television. "I'm taking it day by day."

"But you're healing okay?"

"Healing up just fine. 'Course, I couldn't have done it without a lot of help. People have been real kind to me, especially that young man who saved my life that night.''

Her heart picking up its rhythm, Stephanie asked, ''You mean Derek? Derek Kane?''

''That's him,'' Walter said, his smile revealing pearly-white teeth. ''Now, that's a true Christian man. Pays my medical bills, comes by to see me almost every day, and he's even invited me to go to church with him.''

Stephanie couldn't believe it. She took notes feverishly while Walter Griffin went on and on about the man who'd not only saved his life, but was now determined to help him find a better life.

Needing to know, needing to understand, she asked, ''Why do you think Mr. Kane is doing all of this for you?''

Walter smiled again, then nodded slowly. '''Cause, like I told you, he's a good Christian. Not many people like that in this old world today, that's for sure. I hope you tell everyone that in your story.''

As she sat there, talking with Walter Griffin, Stephanie had to agree, but she couldn't bring herself to speak. For some reason, she wanted to cry. More and more, she was beginning to see that Derek was a rare human being—one who truly followed the word of God by quietly trying to make a difference in people's lives.

"This isn't for a story," she said. "It's just between us. Derek doesn't want any publicity."

"That's a shame. It would make a good story," Walter replied, but his silent, slow nod indicated he understood.

When she'd gotten back to the office and found Derek's message on her voice mail, her heart had filled with joy and excitement. He wanted to have dinner with her, at his place. A sure sign that he was warming up to her after all, and in spite of Glover's intrusive efforts the other night.

Now, as she turned off the motor and climbed out of her car, she had to wonder how many other lost souls Derek had tried to help. How many people had been touched by his kindness, by his gentle urgings, by his need to help his fellow man?

And why wouldn't he let her tell his story?

She couldn't even tell him that she'd talked to Walter Griffin. It would only make Derek think that she couldn't keep her promise to him. She knew she wouldn't use the information she'd gathered unless Glover forced her to get involved, but Derek would never believe that.

So she went to him, with her secrets and her unasked questions, and her doubts, hoping that she could win him over enough to help him if and when the whole story ever did come out. In the meantime, she'd find out everything she could about him—because now she had to know, for herself. For her own peace of mind.

Derek heard the soft knock on the open glass sliding door leading to the deck. "C'mon in," he called.

All around him the doors and windows were thrown open to the pleasant spring night. He couldn't have asked for better weather, or a better date.

As usual, she looked as if she'd just stepped out of a fashion magazine. She wore a light blue linen button-down shirt and sturdy khaki walking shorts. The cameras didn't really do her justice, he decided. "Hello. You're right on time."

"Hi," she said, her smile almost shy. "Thanks for inviting me."

Now, why did he suddenly feel so awkward? Maybe because he was remembering the last time she'd been here and how he'd deliberately kissed her. To scare her away. Yet he'd invited her right back. To see her again. Now he was the scared one.

Yeah, you're real tough, Kane.

Glancing around, hoping to find something to keep him busy, he saw that he'd been too efficient. He'd finished marinating the steaks, and the potatoes and salad were already done. They'd eat on the deck, so he'd wait till later to bring out the utensils.

"It smells wonderful in here," Stephanie said as she strolled across the spacious den and into his kitchen, a bag of cookies from a famous Atlanta department store in one hand. "Chocolate chip and oatmeal," she explained. "Since I ate most of yours last time I was here."

Seeing the label, Derek whistled. "And some of the best chocolate-chip-oatmeal cookies in all of Atlanta. I'm impressed."

Stephanie whirled around. "And so am I. Derek, this place is beautiful. It's more glass than wood, though, isn't it?"

Derek grinned. "I like windows—lots of wide-open spaces and lots of light."

"Did you design this yourself?"

"With a little help from my family."

"Do you have family here?"

He saw the interest on her face, and told himself it was just natural curiosity, nothing more. "No... uh, back in south Georgia. Six brothers and sisters, three of each. I'm the baby."

Her face lit up. "The baby boy of a big family. My, my."

He tossed the dish towel he'd had over his shoulder onto the counter, then grabbed the plate of steaks. "And what's that supposed to mean?"

"Oh, nothing." She leaned over the counter, one brow quirked in a question mark. "You weren't spoiled, were you?"

"Hardly." He leaned across, mocking her position. "We all worked our tails off farming. We always had chores and more chores, and homework and jobs and volunteer work at church. No slackers in the Kane family, no sir.''

"And yet, you're grinning as if you loved every minute of it. Are you still close to your folks?''

"Very." He straightened, balancing the plate with one hand while with his other he indicated a tray with two glasses and a pitcher. "Here, take this iced tea and let's go out onto the deck. I want you to see the sunset over the lake.''

And he wanted to shift the conversation away from himself. He could see the extreme interest in her eyes. He didn't want to doubt her sincerity, but there it was.

"How about you?'' he said as they settled into two Adirondack-style deck chairs to sip their tea while the steaks cooked on the grill. "How about *you* tell *me* your story?''

She sank down, then propped her sandaled feet against the deck floor, her walking shorts revealing tanned, shapely legs. "Dull City. You wouldn't be interested.''

Derek leaned close to give her an intense look. "Try me.''

"Okay, all right. I'm an only child to an older couple. My mother retired a few years ago from teaching at an inner-city school and now she lives in the north Georgia mountains where she grew up, in a modern cabin my father built from the ground up." Her voice softened then. "They always wanted to retire back there."

Derek could see the quietness falling over her, as if she'd just remembered something incredibly sad and personal.

"And your father?"

She looked up then, and out across the lake, her eyes still shuttered, maybe from the burnished sun, maybe from the memories, the blue warring with green. Slipping her sunglasses back on, she said, "He died ten years ago."

Derek sat up to take her hand. "I'm sorry. If you don't want to talk about it—"

"No, it's okay." She flipped her glasses back up on her head. "It was just…his death was such a shock, so brutal. My father was a state trooper. He made a routine traffic stop—the guy's left taillight was broken—and the man got violent. He beat my father so badly that he never regained consciousness."

Derek was on his feet, kneeling in front of her, before he could even think to stop himself. "Stephanie…that's…I'm so sorry."

She took the hands he offered, clinging to him, her eyes misty. "It still gets to me, you know. I loved my father, thought the world of him. He was so big, so strong, I thought nothing could ever harm him and that he would always be there to protect my mother and me." She took a deep breath, held it, closed her eyes, then opened them again to look at Derek. "And then, one night he was just gone. He died on the way to the hospital. Somehow, this big, strapping man had been brutalized by a criminal who'd just been released from prison less than a week before."

Shaking her head, she said, "The man was carrying drugs. He didn't want to go back to prison. They say he matched my father in size and that...that Daddy gave a valiant fight...and he did stay alert long enough to radio for help before the guy drove away. So at least they caught him. He won't be getting out of prison for a very long time, but that won't bring my daddy back."

They sat there silent, still holding hands, Derek on his knees, Stephanie sitting forward in her chair. Behind them the sun danced across the water, turning everything amber and bronze as it moved behind the tree line.

Stephanie glanced toward the sun, then smiled shakily. "I'm okay. Really, I'm fine."

Derek watched her face. She was washed in a golden aura, her skin, her hair, her eyes. And she looked so innocent, so young, so alone, sitting there. This was a side of her none of her viewers had ever seen, he'd wager. This was a side of her he'd never forget.

He reached up to brush a loose curl off her temple. "I'm sorry, honey. That's rough."

She smiled then, a crooked bittersweet effort that melted his heart and made him want to hold her and protect her.

"That's why I became a reporter," she told him. "I wanted to go into law enforcement, but…my mother couldn't deal with that. So I thought being a reporter would be the next best thing—you know, tracking down the bad guys, exposing crime, searching for the truth."

He nodded, understanding her intense need for justice, her intense need to keep on searching, even when she probably already had the answers.

He'd once had that same need.

Derek saw the pain in her eyes and wished he could erase it forever, but sadly, he couldn't help Stephanie fight these demons. He couldn't help, because he'd known the same kind of pain, felt the same kind of rage and raw, tattered emotion. And it had come close to destroying his life.

But he couldn't tell her about that. He couldn't let her know just how much he understood exactly what she was going through. To do so would mean he'd have to reveal the whole ugly truth, and then she'd see him for what he really was. She'd see that he wasn't worthy of being called a hero or a Good Samaritan. He wasn't worthy of anything at all.

Still holding her hand, Derek thought back over what Stephanie had just told him, a sick dread pooling like stagnant water in the pit of his stomach.

Her father had been a state patrol—a cop.

Derek sat there watching her face, looking into her eyes, and wondered what she would think if she knew that he'd once been a police officer himself.

Chapter Eight

His whole mood had changed.

Stephanie sat in a wooden swing down on the dock, drinking coffee while she watched Derek fishing for bream off the pier. Lazarus strolled along the wide dock, his tail wagging each time Derek threw out his line. Wondering what she'd said or done to make Derek clam up again, she thought back over the evening.

They'd had a wonderful dinner. He sure could cook a steak to perfection. But Derek had been awfully quiet after she'd told him about her father's death. Maybe he just didn't know how to console someone who was still grieving. Maybe he thought she should be over it by now. She wanted to tell him that she was doing better—after all, it had been a long time. But some wounds took longer to heal, especially when she'd been so recently cast into a scenario much like what had happened to her father. The memories had all come rushing back.

But after having told Derek about her father's death, she hadn't dwelled on it. The conversation had moved on to other things. They'd talked about the weather, about the traffic into the city, about Lazarus, about the lake. Normal, mundane things. In fact, Derek had almost made it a point to turn the conversation toward small talk.

During dinner she'd told him about going to see Walter Griffin. She'd felt it best to be honest with Derek about that, at least. But maybe that had been a bad idea.

"Are you angry that I'm going to do a follow-up story on the mugging?" she asked him now, her voice echoing out over the lake.

Derek turned from the line he'd just cast to glance back at her. "Not really. Not as long as you leave my name out of it."

"I told you I would." She waited for some sort of reaction, but Derek only pivoted back around to stare down into the murky lake waters. Hoping to open up the conversation again, she said, "It was awfully nice of you to pay Mr. Griffin's hospital bill, though. Just one more reason to let the public know the entire story."

That got his attention. Hitching his long cane fishing pole to a metal holder on a nearby post, he strolled over to sit beside her in the spacious swing. Lazarus whined and plopped down at their feet, clearly frustrated that there wasn't room for him in the swing.

"I thought we'd cleared up all of that," Derek told her, his expression closed and wary.

"We have." She sighed, then swung her foot. "Why don't you want people to know how kind you are?"

He sighed right back. "Maybe because sometimes people take advantage of that sort of thing. Look, I just don't see the need to broadcast all over Atlanta that I helped someone out. People help each other every day, and it doesn't make the news."

"My point exactly," she replied, smacking a hand against the rusty chains. "Good news—something we all could use."

He angled his head to stare over at her. "But you usually go after the tough stories—criminal investigations, murder and mayhem, exposing corrupt politicians. Why is this story so important to you?"

Stephanie heard the edge in his voice. He wanted her to drop this completely, but she needed him to understand why it *was* so important to her. "I guess because seeing that old man get beaten up only reminded me of what happened to my father. I wish someone like you had been there for him that night."

His features softened then. "I understand about

your father, but telling the world about me won't bring him back.''

"No, but it might encourage others to get more involved, to help their fellow human beings in a time of need. You've gone beyond the call of duty—you're trying to help Walter Griffin find a better life.''

Needing to understand, she shifted gears. "And why weren't you at the hearing? Don't you even want to know what happened? Those two boys got off with two years' probation and community service. I just wish—''

He put a finger to her lips. "I'm not going to change my mind on this, Stephanie. I didn't attend the hearing because I don't want or need the publicity and because I figured those two might finagle a plea bargain. So if you're here to try and persuade me to step forward, you can leave now.''

Taking his hand away, Stephanie held it in her own. "Is that what you think? That while you're fishing for bream, I'm still fishing for a story?''

"Are you gonna deny it?''

She dropped his hand to stare out over the lake. Taking a deep breath, she inhaled all the fragrances of the earth. The scent of lemony magnolia blossoms warred with the more earthy scent of decaying plants and fishy lake waters. "I guess I can't deny my curiosity, or the need to find out the truth about you. I don't see this sort of thing every day, you know.

But it's like I told you—it's more personal now. I want to know for me, Derek. Not for some story.''

He pulled her chin around, then held his finger on her cheekbone. ''Look, there is no story. I...I just had a bad run-in with the press a few years back, and now I'm camera shy. On the other hand, if you're here because you find being with me irresistible and because you're starting to like me a little, then you can stay.''

Stephanie grinned reluctantly, then slapped his hand away. ''Okay, that I can't deny.''

She longed to ask him what he'd done to make the press come after him, but decided he wasn't ready to talk about that, obviously. He still didn't trust her enough. Somehow, she wanted to win his trust, maybe more than she wanted to know about his past.

Pushing the swing into a faster movement, Derek winked at her. ''So, you do like me and I'm irresistible?''

She laughed as the swing made an arc through the cool evening breeze, Lazarus chasing it as they swished through the air. ''Well, your steaks are irresistible. I never could turn down a good square meal.''

He paid her back by taking them even higher into the air. Screaming, she begged for mercy. ''I'm going to be sick if you don't slow this thing down.''

After a few more seconds of swinging too fast,

Derek eased the rickety old swing to a slow whine. "I'm glad you came."

"Me, too," she told him. "And I'm glad we talked about…things. I just thought since you'd gotten so quiet on me again, maybe you were angry about me going to see Walter. But, Derek, your secret is safe with me. If you don't want anyone to know what you've done, then they won't. Not from me, anyway."

Derek turned serious again, then rose from the swing to check his line. "I'm sorry. I'm not much of a conversationalist to begin with, and…well, I've got some things on my mind, things I have to work through. And I have my reasons for remaining anonymous in all of this. But it's nothing for you to worry about, okay?"

"Okay."

"Good. Now, can we talk about something besides what happened the other night? Can we just concentrate on getting to know each other and forget about this story?"

"Yes," she said, her tone quiet. "I'd like that."

And she'd also like to know why he was acting so distant, so secretive, and how he'd managed to find out about the plea bargain for the two juveniles. Something was bothering him and she could only guess that it had to do with his personal life, maybe with having *her* in his personal life.

Very much aware that she was attracted to a man

about whom she knew nothing, Stephanie couldn't help but think that she knew enough. She knew he was a good man, a man any woman would be proud to know. She knew he'd been hurt, somehow, by someone, and that hurt had caused him to turn away, to live here in seclusion, to work with the earth more than with the people who inhabited it.

As she watched him, she was once again assaulted by that familiar feeling. Derek reminded her of someone, something, but whatever or whoever it was, it was right out of her grasp. His mannerisms, his actions, only reinforced these feelings. Maybe somewhere in her years as a reporter here in Atlanta, she'd come across Derek before. Glancing up at him, she had a thought. She'd go through the archives back at work, check to see if he'd been in the public eye before—a story of some sort, a face in a crowd, maybe a witness to some other, bigger, more dangerous crime? Was that why he was hiding out here?

Had she seen Derek somewhere before?

I think I would have remembered him, she told herself as she left the swing to get down on the planked dock with Lazarus.

For the first time it occurred to Stephanie that by trying to reveal Derek's identity as the Good Samaritan, she might be putting his life in danger. If that were the case, why didn't he just tell her?

She'd told him she was dropping the whole thing.

But it wouldn't hurt to check, just for her own peace of mind. It wouldn't hurt at all.

He didn't want to hurt Stephanie.

Derek looked out over Miss Nadine's garden, wishing he'd slept better the night before. But thoughts of his conversation with Stephanie had made that impossible.

Today was a big day. Mowing day. With an estate this size, it would take all day just to get the riding mower over the main areas of the yard before he could take the weed chopper and work around the perimeters.

He didn't need the distraction of worrying about his growing feelings for Stephanie Maguire. He didn't need the distraction of having to train two new part-time helpers. He didn't need anything or anyone getting in the way of his peaceful, private, tranquil, unassuming existence.

But it was all there, glaring him in the face just as surely as the morning sun was glaring down on the dewy grass. And Derek knew in his heart that sooner or later he would have to tell Stephanie his story. From beginning to end. With all the bitter details.

"Not just yet, Lord," he said into the wind. "Not yet. I...I think I'm falling for her. Just let me enjoy getting to know her. Let me be free and at peace for a while longer. Let me try to win her over, before she finds out the truth.''

Why he wanted this so desperately, Derek couldn't explain. He should just leave Stephanie Maguire alone. He should just tell her that he couldn't see her again. That whatever they might have had together was over.

That had been his original plan. To convince her to back off, then to leave her alone and hope that she'd do the same for him. But instead, he'd invited her to dance with him, had invited her to come to his home, to sit in his swing, her long legs curled up underneath her as if she'd always belonged there.

Instead, he'd fallen and fallen hard. And now it was way too late to push her away.

Her father was killed in the line of duty.

That thought went through Derek's mind, whirling like a noisy lawnmower.

Her father had been a lawman.

Derek wished he'd known that before he'd ever gotten involved with Stephanie Maguire. And he wished he'd told her right up front that he'd once been a policeman himself.

Now he'd have to walk a fine line, hoping she wouldn't find out, hoping that if she did, she'd understand why he had kept it all a secret.

Either way, she'd wind up getting hurt.

Either way, he'd wind up regretting that he'd carried this too far.

* * *

"I've gone as far back as possible," Stephanie told the production assistant who'd helped her filter through tape after tape, searching through different stories, hoping to find something about Derek. "I guess this is one hunch that isn't going to pay off."

It didn't help that James Glover appeared behind her in the darkened production room at just that moment.

"Whatcha doing?"

"Looking for Derek Kane," the assistant, a young woman who had a definite crush on James, said with all the innocence of someone who was tired and hungry for lunch.

"Oh, really?" James's interest perked up considerably. "I knew it! Stef, what gives with this man, anyway? And don't tell me you're just hoping to get a better angle on planting petunias."

Stephanie moaned silently, then turned to the confused young woman at her side. "Sheli, go on to lunch. I'll finish this up. Thanks for your help."

Sheli didn't have to be told twice. Obviously glad to be out from under the demanding arm of WNT's workaholic reporter, she practically ran from the small room.

Glover waited until the heavy door closed behind them, then turned to Stephanie. "Tell me everything."

"I can't," Stephanie replied, her eyes scanning a newsreel from five years before. "It's personal."

"Oh, so you *do* have a thing for our master gardener?"

"Yes," she admitted. Maybe if she laid it all out for Glover, he'd back off. He didn't go for the mushy stuff. "I'm just intrigued by him. And I think I've seen him somewhere before."

"That's a mighty big curiosity," Glover commented, eyeing the date and label of the tape. "Criminal investigations."

"I don't want to date a known felon," she said in a flippant tone. "Besides, I've already checked that angle. He's got a clean record. No criminal activity or incarceration that I can find."

At least, that's what the official record said. His story about being born in south Georgia checked out. And his business was legitimate—Derek really was a landscaper. And before that, he'd held various odd jobs here and there since arriving in Atlanta. From all indications, Derek was just a normal working man. Just an all-around nice guy. With a big secret.

"Then why are you still searching?" Glover said, leaning over to stare down at her.

"I just want to cover all my bases. I…I really like him and I want to be sure. You know my record with guys."

"Yeah, but I've never known you to do such heavy research. Usually you just dump them after the first date."

Wishing he'd take the hint and leave, Stephanie shot him a sweet smile. "Well, this one is different. Because I do like him so very much, I want to be completely sure I have all the facts."

"And you expect me to believe this?"

Pushed to the limit, Stephanie threw up a hand. "No, but I expect you to just go away and take care of your own business. Please, Glover, trust me on this. It's not anything for you to be bothered about. No big scoop, no major story. Just something that involves my personal life, which I'd like to keep personal, if you don't mind."

"Oh, I don't mind," Glover said, backing toward the door. "But I know you're not telling me everything. I can do my own research, though. See what's shaking."

"No!" Angry that he'd pushed her to despair, Stephanie got up to face him. "I'm asking you nicely to keep your nose out of this, Glover. Don't make me have to go to Claire with this."

"Oh, wow. It's even bigger than I thought."

With that, Glover was out the door, his condescending grin shining from ear to ear.

He wouldn't give up; he wouldn't quit until he had the story. And there was no way Stephanie could stop him. They'd competed on too many levels, too many times.

So now she had the added stress of finding out everything before Glover did, and putting it all together before Derek found out she even knew anything.

"Lord, how am I going to pull this off?" she whispered. "How can I do this? I can't stop now—Glover's on to me. I have to find out the truth, to protect Derek if nothing else."

Telling herself to calm down, Stephanie went over the facts again. Derek Kane was who he said he was, at least. He didn't have a criminal record, but there was a definite lack of information regarding his whereabouts before he moved to Atlanta. He had connections with the police department—at least, he'd persuaded them to keep his name out of this investigation. And he didn't want anyone in Atlanta to know that he even existed.

Could he be an informant of some sort, working undercover?

That possibility had crossed her mind more than once.

But…why would he assume the role of a landscaper if he was working for the government or the police?

Suddenly Stephanie had another idea. What if Derek was trying to get to someone really big—someone high up in the local government? That would explain his working for some of the most influential people in Atlanta.

"I'll go talk to Miss Nadine," she told herself as

she grabbed an apple and rushed toward the elevators.

Nadine Hamilton would never hire someone she didn't know about. The woman was a stickler for honesty and integrity and she had positively glowed when telling Glover about Derek's work. Miss Nadine had to know something, anything, that could help ease this growing unease Stephanie couldn't shake.

And Miss Nadine would talk, off the record. She didn't talk to just anyone, but she'd talk to Stephanie. Stephanie would make sure of that.

And maybe she'd find out what she needed to know.

Before Glover and the rest of Atlanta found out.

Chapter Nine

"Now, what brings the lovely Stephanie Maguire back to my home so soon?"

Nadine Hamilton poured iced tea from a shimmering crystal pitcher that, as she'd so proudly informed Stephanie earlier when she'd escorted her into a front parlor where a maid had been setting out refreshments, had been in her family for over one hundred and fifty years. And so had the matching goblet she carefully handed to Stephanie.

Praying she wouldn't drop the heavy and obviously priceless crystal, Stephanie took a tentative sip of the deliciously sweet, mint-and-lemon-laced tea and smiled up at her hostess. "I just wanted to drop by to follow up on the interview we did the other night. By the way, I really enjoyed the reception, Miss Nadine. You must have the loveliest garden in all of Atlanta, next to Calloway Gardens, of course."

"Thank you. My cousin married a Calloway," Nadine replied as she sat on a floral-covered chair, her back straight, her dress fluffed around her tiny ankles. Then, her expression changing from prim to precise, she touched a finger to the strand of pearls nestled in the lace at her collar and said, "Okay, darlin', let's cut to the chase. I get the impression you aren't here to talk about roses and peat moss."

Flustered but not defeated, Stephanie placed her half-full goblet of tea on the white lace doily supplied on the nearby Chippendale table. There was no beating around the bush with Miss Nadine.

"I'm here regarding your gardener, Miss Nadine," she said in what she hoped was a businesslike tone. "I thought it was intriguing that he designed and landscaped your garden and several others along the tour. I'd like to do a feature story on him—you know, a lighthearted piece on his love for his work, and his immense talent. It would be perfect for these nice spring days when everyone is working outside anyway. But…the man's hard to pin down."

Miss Nadine's blue eyes narrowed suspiciously. "Mr. Kane? He keeps to himself. Might not be willing to talk to you."

Stephanie smiled, then tapped her pen on her notepad. "I was hoping you could help me out. What do you know about Mr. Kane?"

Nadine Hamilton sat straight-backed in her chair, then looked down her nose at Stephanie. "I know all I need to know. He's a good gardener and he minds his own business."

She stopped there, then took a dainty sip of her own tea. With a pleasant smile, she gave Stephanie a look of dismissal, as if to say, "And that's all you need to know, too."

"How did you meet him?" Stephanie asked, determined not to be intimidated.

Miss Nadine carefully placed her tea on the table, then fussed with a fresh arrangement of magnolia blossoms floating in a fluted glass bowl full of water. The lemony scent of the big white blooms rose out into the air, while Miss Nadine obviously debated whether to talk anymore or not.

Giving Stephanie another penetrating look, she finally said, "A good friend of mine, Louise Thomas, the woman who nursed my dear husband before his death, introduced me to him, told me he had a way with plants and flowers. He needed a job and I needed a better, more dependable gardener. So far, things have worked out rather nicely. I trust Mr. Kane, and we have a mutual respect for each other." She paused, straightened the knife-blade pleats in her cream silk dress, then looked straight into Stephanie's eyes. "And I won't talk about the man behind his back."

Feeling as if she'd been properly reprimanded,

Stephanie tried again. "I mean no disrespect. I'm truly interested in him—his occupation, his way with flowers and shrubs. Your garden has never looked better."

"How do you know? This is the first time you've ever attended the opening reception, to my knowledge."

She *would* remember that, Stephanie thought in a brief panic.

"But this is the first time you've held it at your home. Wasn't it held at the Piedmont Riding Club before?"

"Several times. And at various other private homes here and there. I don't recall seeing you at any of those locations, however."

Trying mighty hard not to squirm, Stephanie leaned forward. "I do apologize for not being able to attend before this year. But…once I saw your backyard, well, I just had to follow up. I'm amazed at all the color—the roses, azaleas, magnolias—"

Nadine held up a wrinkled, bejeweled hand. "I know what all's growing in my garden, dear. But I don't think you really want to hear about flowers. I saw you talking with Mr. Kane at the reception."

Feeling foolish, Stephanie lowered her head. "Well, yes, we did talk briefly—"

"And disappeared together for a mighty long time. I know because that other reporter, Gomer,

Glover, whatever his name was, was running around like a cocker spaniel looking for you."

"James Glover—he helped me cover the reception. Our boss believes in the team concept. And yes, he wanted to interview Derek that night."

Miss Nadine lifted her chin. "Derek, is it? My, my, seems you two did get further acquainted. If I recall correctly from that night, when Mr. Kane spotted you in the garden he told me you'd met before."

Surprised that Derek had even spoken about her, Stephanie nodded. "We did—but just briefly. He's a very nice man."

"And nice-looking, to boot."

"Yes, that, too."

Miss Nadine crossed her hands in her lap, then gave an eloquent shrug. "He could use some companionship in his life."

Stephanie tried not to appear too interested. "Really? So…he's not attached or anything?" She had to know. Maybe Derek had someone else, or maybe he was still in love with someone else, still carrying a torch.

Nadine shook her head. "Single. Completely alone, except for that mutt Lazarus."

"You've met Lazarus?"

The old woman's head shot up. "*You've* met Lazarus?"

Stephanie groaned inwardly. She was in way over

her head. "I...uh, yes." She couldn't lie to Miss Nadine. It just wasn't possible, not with the woman staring her down like a Sunday school teacher.

"Maybe you'd better tell me exactly what's going on here," Miss Nadine said, her tone soft and encouraging. "Child, if you want to court Mr. Kane, why don't you just say so?"

"Court?" Stephanie had to smile at the endearing quality of that old-fashioned word. "I don't know about courting him—I'd just like to get to know him better."

Rising off her chair, Miss Nadine held out a hand to Stephanie. "Well, you certainly can't do that by questioning a senile old woman, now, can you?"

"I guess I just needed some advice," Stephanie said on a defeated tone. Maybe she could win Miss Nadine over if the older woman saw herself as a matchmaker. "Derek doesn't open up much."

"He's a man of few words—a quality I greatly admire," Nadine said, her tone pointed, her hand squeezing Stephanie's.

"So how do you suggest I go about learning more about him?"

Nadine guided Stephanie down a long, cool central hallway, past polished side tables and brocade chairs, to the back of the big house. Unsure where they were headed, Stephanie was afraid to ask questions. But the roar of a lawn mower caught her attention.

Looking out the paneled double doors, she recognized the rounded veranda Derek had been standing on the night of the reception. And out in the far corner of the sweeping lawn, she saw the man himself on a riding lawn mower.

He was wearing a faded blue T-shirt with the arms cut out at the shoulders and an old pair of cutoff blue jeans. A colorful bandanna sweatband cut a swath across his forehead, making him look almost savage. In tux or T-shirt, the man took her breath away.

"He's here," she said, her voice catching on the intake of breath.

"Yes, he is. Go on out. Since you two seem to be in some sort of courting ritual anyway, why wait?"

Stephanie turned to the woman at her side. "Miss Nadine, I'm sorry."

"For what?"

"I came here hoping to pry information about Derek out of you. You see, I'm a reporter. It's the only way I know how to find out things—to ask, to dig, to search for the truth. But I shouldn't have tried to trick you that way. I hope you won't say anything to Derek about this."

The older woman smiled, then patted Stephanie's hand. "You didn't trick me, not for one second. When you've been on the earth as long as I have, you learn a few tricks yourself. Honey, it's written all over your face why you're really here."

Surprised, Stephanie felt sheepish. "And you don't mind?"

Nadine scoffed, then waved a hand in the air. "Mind? I'm thrilled to pieces that Mr. Kane has the possibility of someone pretty and sweet in his life. He's a good Christian, and he deserves someone to love. I'm counting on you, so don't let me—or him—down."

Stephanie felt the weight of Miss Nadine's blessing as well as the weight of her challenge. "Do you know why he seems so..."

"Sad? Quiet? Reserved?"

Stephanie nodded.

"I think our Mr. Kane has been deeply hurt, but instead of being bitter about it, he turned to God for love and support, and for forgiveness. I don't question that kind of quiet faith. I just accept it as part of God's healing grace. Maybe you should try that, too."

Stephanie looked at the woman at her side, tears building up in her eyes. "I want to have that kind of unquestioning faith, but...it's hard."

"You don't want to give your heart over to anyone, including the Lord?"

"Yes, maybe that's it. I was raised in a Christian home, went to church all my life, but I'm afraid."

Nadine looked out over her garden, then turned

back to Stephanie. "There is a passage in Second Timothy—'For God has not given us a spirit of fear, but of power and of love and of a sound mind.' Do you know the passage?"

"I remember it, yes," Stephanie replied.

"Then cling to it, dear. You have a spirit, a wonderful, caring spirit, and you seem to have a sound mind. We can all see that every night in the stories you tell. You care about people. Use that spirit for good, use that spirit for love, real love. And don't be afraid to turn your heart over to the Lord, or over to love."

Grinning then, she added with a wink, "You don't want to miss out on love, darlin'. Especially with a man like Mr. Kane. He's a rare commodity— a man who is faithful to that which he holds dear."

"He's a hero," Stephanie said, almost to herself.

But Miss Nadine heard her. "Not a hero. Just a man trying to find his way. A good man."

In the next instant, everything they'd just discussed swept out of Stephanie's mind. As she stood there with Miss Nadine, watching Derek on the riding lawn mower, two other workers approached him. He switched off the machine, got up and stood talking quietly to them. And Stephanie recognized them both.

"I can't believe it," Stephanie said, rushing past Miss Nadine to open the door and hurry down the veranda steps.

"What's the matter?" Nadine called, right on her heels.

"It's the two teenagers," Stephanie said. "The two who mugged Walter Griffin."

"What are you talking about?" Nadine shouted after her.

But Stephanie didn't reply. She was too shocked. What on earth were those two juvenile delinquents doing here in Miss Nadine's garden?

Then suddenly it all made perfect sense.

Derek had taken the two under his wing. This was their community service.

And he hadn't even bothered to tell her about it.

Derek glanced up to see what all the ruckus was up at the house. That's when he saw Stephanie, wearing a tan linen business suit, running down the steps, with Miss Nadine close on her heels.

"Oh, great," he moaned, then glared at his two surly companions. "Boys, I'm only going to say this once. You do not want to mess with the two women approaching us, so let me do all the talking, all right?"

"What's up with them, man?"

Derek looked at Marco Stanley, the younger of the two, and shook his head. The kid had attitude from his untied sneakers to the skullcap he wore on his head. And Derek had promised the judge and the D.A. that he'd crack that attitude by summer's end.

Lifting up a prayer for patience and guidance, Derek stood close to Marco. "Well, the older one owns this entire estate, and the young one—she's a reporter for the most watched newscast in Atlanta. She can make you or break you, buddy. Trust me—this I know."

"That's Stephanie Maguire." Nathan Hayes, older, even tougher, his head shaved to make him look like a pro wrestler, placed his massive arms across his chest and turned back to Derek with a suspicious eye. "Ah, man, don't you remember— she caught us that night. She called the police! Is she gonna interview us, put us on the news, make an example of us or somethin'?"

"Now, there's a thought," Derek said. But again he shook his head. "Just stay quiet and let me take care of this situation."

By that time, Stephanie had made her way through the sprinkler system, obviously oblivious to the mist glistening on her crisp suit.

"Derek," she said, her eyes scanning the two teens standing beside him.

"Hello, Stephanie." He felt the urge to shield the boys from her intense gaze. "What brings you out here on such a fine day?"

"What are you doing with these two?" she said by way of an answer, her taupe pump tapping impatiently against grass clippings.

"Hey, lady, back off," Marco said with a roll of

his hips. "We got community service. We're stuck with him for the summer."

Derek watched as Stephanie's expression went from confused to infuriated. Bearing down on Marco, she said, "Do you remember me?"

Marco bobbed his dark head. "Sure do. Why'd you snitch on us, anyway?"

Stephanie looked at Derek, then back to the boy. "Why? You were beating up a helpless old man. And if I had things my way, you'd be behind bars instead of standing around out here in this lovely garden."

Nathan stepped forward then. "We ain't been standing around." Motioning to Derek, he added in a snarl of broken English, "He don't give us time to catch our breath before we're diggin' and waterin' all over again."

"It's called work," Derek told him. "And you're lucky that the judge didn't throw you both behind bars like Miss Maguire here suggested."

"Lucky us," Marco said, rolling his eyes.

"Lucky you," Stephanie told them, her hands on her hips. "I just don't get it, Derek. After all the times we've talked, you never once mentioned this. You certainly know how to pull those strings down at the police department, and you obviously convinced the district attorney that these two can be saved."

"Their public defender did the convincing,"

Derek explained. "They're on probation and being closely watched by their probation officer and everyone else involved. We're trying to save them, Stephanie."

"And you felt this intense need to be a Good Samaritan again by getting involved?"

"Call it what you like, but I got involved because I believe they need help," Derek tried to explain. "I'm taking full responsibility for them over the next couple of months."

Nathan interrupted, "Hey, man, we're standing right here. Don't talk about us like we don't even exist."

Giving the boys a hard stare, Derek added, "Even if I have to sit on them to talk some sense into them."

"I think it's very noble of you," Miss Nadine said, coming up from the rear. Stopping to catch her breath, she sent a quieting look around the small cluster gathered in her yard. "I don't know the circumstances surrounding these two fine gentlemen's waywardness, but I highly commend trying to salvage their rotten souls."

Pointing a finger at Marco, she asked, "Son, do you know the Lord?"

Clearly nonplussed, Marco stepped back and scratched his head through his skullcap. "My mama goes to church, yeah. But the Lord ain't done much for me lately."

"It's yes, ma'am, and I suggest you start attending church with your mama, so you can see what the Lord has in store for you."

What followed was much more than a moment of silence. Derek watched as the old woman, armed with the righteousness of God's word, stared down the defiant youth armed with attitude and too many hard knocks.

Righteousness won out. Marco shifted his big feet, tried to form a frown, finally gave up under the scrutinizing glare from Miss Nadine's frosty blue eyes, then grunted and mumbled underneath his breath.

"Yes, ma'am," he replied, taking his cap off in an automatic gesture of respect, his head down.

Miss Nadine lifted his chin with a withered finger. "Look at that handsome face. Look at that beautifully rounded head. Why do you insist on hiding your brains under that hot cap all summer?"

Marco gave Derek a panicked look.

Derek shrugged. "I tried to warn you."

The boy glared again, but didn't dare move his head. "I guess I could leave it in the truck."

"Good idea. If the sun bothers you, wear a lighter hat."

"Yes, ma'am."

Nathan snorted his disdain, which only brought Miss Nadine's acute attention to him. "And you, young man. What's your excuse for being here to-day? What'd you do?''

Nathan ran a hand over his shaved head, then glared over at her. "I don't have to talk to you."

Derek stepped up then, his face about an inch away from Nathan's. "Answer the lady."

Nathan shifted, tugged at his baggy pants, then pawed the dirt. Finally he tilted his head at a stubborn angle and said, "These two caught us picking on an old man, is all. We weren't doing anything—just having some fun."

"You almost killed him," Stephanie replied, disgust evident in her words. Stepping closer to Nathan, she asked, "Should I bring you pictures of Walter Griffin from his hospital bed, let you see what your 'just having fun' did to that poor man?" Waving a hand in the air, she said, "If Derek hadn't come along when he did—"

Then she stopped, looked over at Miss Nadine, glanced back at Derek, an apology poised on her lips.

Derek wanted to tell her to just be quiet, but from the expression on Miss Nadine's face, he knew the woman had figured it all out.

"It was you, wasn't it, Mr. Kane?" she asked, her hands now folded in front of her. "You were the Good Samaritan Miss Maguire reported on a few days ago?"

"Yes, ma'am," Derek said, a long, tired sigh

leaving his body. "I came along when Stephanie was trying to save Walter Griffin from these two. We both saw the whole thing, but they copped a plea with the D.A. and…through an arrangement with him and the judge, I offered to *recondition* them."

"Recondition them. I like that," Miss Nadine said before turning to Stephanie. "You left out some things, child, regarding how you and Mr. Kane first met."

"Yes, I did," Stephanie admitted, "because Derek insisted he wanted to remain anonymous. But then, he neglected to tell me just how involved he'd actually become with this whole case." She pointed at Derek, her expression full of accusation. "How did they manage a plea bargain, anyway?"

Derek glanced at the boys. "Want me to tell her?"

Marco shrugged, his cap still clutched in one hand. He was the follower, and Derek could tell already that he was beginning to crack under the intense scrutiny of someone actually caring about him. But he was fighting it. The boy looked toward Nathan for some sort of sign as to what to do or say.

Nathan shifted from foot to foot. "It don't matter. We're dead meat if they find us."

"If who finds you?" Stephanie asked.

Derek sighed again, then threw his hands down at his sides. "These two were ordered to find someone, anyone, and beat them up. It was part of an initiation into a street gang. And once they passed that test, they had orders to do even worse the next time.''

Miss Nadine's hand flew to her throat. ''Oh, my.''

Stephanie's gaze moved from one boy to the next, understanding dawning in her eyes as she stated the obvious. ''And you agreed to turn in gang members in order to save your own hides, right?''

''We didn't want to do it,'' Marco insisted, a genuine fear centered in his hazel eyes. ''We didn't want to beat up anybody, or kill anyone, but they threatened us.'' He was silent a minute, then added on a low voice, ''And once we got into it, we sorta lost it, you know. We…we didn't mean to hurt him that bad.''

''Yeah,'' Nathan added, his own expression grim. ''But the cops, they said we'd go to jail with some really bad people, even worse than any gang members we'd ever met. They scared us into snitching, and now—'' he shrugged again ''—we're dead if they find us.''

''You have every reason to be afraid,'' Stephanie said. ''I saw some pretty unscrupulous people hanging out at your hearing the other day.''

That put new threads of fear on both of the boys' faces. ''They were trying to find out where they were taking us,'' Nathan said on what sounded like a quiver. ''They'll track us down.''

"I told you, they aren't going to harm either of you," Derek said, sending Stephanie a warning look to hush her up. "First of all, the police have picked up the leaders for questioning, and they're watching the others, just waiting for them to make a wrong move."

"That don't stop 'em," Marco said, his hands arcing up in the air. "They just keep adding new members. The police can't stop 'em."

"Then I will," Derek assured him. "I told you both, I'm going to protect you, and together we're going to find a way for both of you to come out of this." Turning to Stephanie, he said, "And that's why they're spending the summer with me, at my lake house, where they'll be safe and supervised."

He hated the distrust, the hurt he saw in her eyes. But maybe it was for the best. He certainly couldn't be with her, or tell her everything she wanted to know.

As if reading his mind, she said, "Why didn't you just level with me, Derek? Is this why you didn't want your name on the news? Did you plan on this all along, from the minute you stepped in to intervene?"

"No," he told her, frustration coloring his voice. "I decided to do this after talking to the cops and the D.A. I know a few people on the force, okay? And I know that there are a lot of teens out there who are afraid and unsure. The statistics point to intervention as a way of saving some of them. I wanted to help these two before they made an even bigger mistake.''

"So, is this your thing, then? Is this why you're so secretive about yourself? Do you work with the cops, undercover, to bust up gangs, to break up drug rings? Are you an informant?''

Derek ran his hand through his hair. "No, I'm not an informant. I just try to help out here and there, and yes, it's part of the reason I didn't want you to do a story on me.''

Miss Nadine spoke up then. "As I said earlier, very noble. But very dangerous, too.''

Misunderstanding, Derek pivoted to her. "Miss Nadine, you're in no danger having these two here. Between Lazarus and me, they won't dare do anything to disrespect you, and the gang they were involved in has no idea where they are. They think these two are locked away somewhere, waiting to do their community service.''

"Oh, I'm not concerned for my own welfare,'' Miss Nadine replied. "I have an excellent security system installed all over the grounds and house. But I do worry about you and these boys.''

"No need,'' Derek told her.

"They have spies everywhere,'' Marco said. "They'll know we got off easy.''

"But they don't know where you are, and by the time they figure anything out, the cops will have busted them up,'' Derek said. Then he put a finger to Marco's chest. ''Listen, I promised I would protect you and that's just exactly what I'm going to do, day and night.''

Checking his watch, he placed his arms across his chest. ''Now, ladies, you both have your answers. And we really need to get back to work. We've still got a lot of yard to mow and clear.''

Miss Nadine gave Stephanie a knowing glance, then slowly turned back toward the house. ''Well, I for one have had quite enough excitement for one morning. I have some phone calls to make.'' Then she turned back to Derek. ''But your mission will not be amongst my topics of discussion, Mr. Kane.''

''I appreciate your discretion, and your understanding,'' Derek told her.

Then he turned to Stephanie. ''And I'd appreciate the same from you.''

Stephanie watched as Marco and Nathan begin raking grass clippings into a pile, Lazarus following them like the watchdog he obviously was trained to be.

''This story just keeps twisting and shifting,'' she said, her tone quiet, her eyes centered on Derek. ''And you continue to amaze me. Next you'll have them both in church with you, singing hymns of praise.''

Derek grinned then, relaxing just a little after the tension of the morning. ''As a matter of fact, that's exactly where we'll be this Sunday. A little church out near the lake, far away from the inner city where these two grew up.''

He stepped over to a flower bed and broke off a single yellow rose blossom, then handed it to her. ''And you're welcome to join us.''

Chapter Ten

Stephanie fell in love with the little church. Aptly called the Church of Flowery Branch, the building was quaint and old-fashioned, complete with pine benches, aged hymnals and fresh bright orange and yellow daylilies taken right from the grounds. Ceiling fans and opened windows brought in the Sunday-morning breezes, while organ music enticed the small congregation to enter the double doors and gather to worship.

"I can't believe I'm doing this," Stephanie mumbled to herself as she entered the coolness of the paneled church to search out Derek. Smiling, she thought she'd gone to a lot of unsavory places to get to the bottom of a story, but never before had she thought of going to church just to get information.

Maybe the Lord was trying to tell her something.

Seeing Derek sitting up front with an older African-American woman and a young girl in a wheelchair, Stephanie mustered her courage and started up the aisle, hoping her floral sundress was appropriate. At least it would prove to be cool, since the church had no air-conditioning.

Derek turned at the sound of her high-heeled sandals tapping against the polished wooden floor.

"Stephanie."

He seemed surprised to see her. As if maybe he hadn't really expected her to show up. And she almost hadn't. She'd talked herself out of it several times during the night. But curiosity killed the cat, and apparently always got the best of her reporter's instincts. She had to come.

And now that she saw the man who'd put more than one kink in her otherwise staid life, she was glad she'd made the effort. He looked great in his short-sleeved shirt, khakis and casual tie. "Hello, Derek. Hope I'm not late."

"No. We're just getting started. C'mon and sit next to me."

When the woman by his side looked up, smiling, Stephanie waited for Derek to introduce them. He seemed to hesitate, then nodded toward Stephanie. "Louise, this is Stephanie Maguire. I think I mentioned her to you."

"You certainly did," the woman named Louise

said, reaching out to shake Stephanie's hand. "How you doing, sugar?"

"Fine," Stephanie replied, wondering just what exactly Derek had said about her.

"This is Louise Thomas," Derek continued, still hesitant. Then he turned to the little girl sitting in the wheelchair. "And this is her granddaughter, Kendra."

Stephanie could tell these two people were important to Derek. And this was Louise—the Louise Miss Nadine had mentioned? This woman knew Derek, had recommended him to Miss Nadine. She would certainly have some answers regarding his past.

"Hello, Kendra," Stephanie said, taking the little girl's slender hand. "How are you?"

"I'm doing okay," Kendra said, a smile cresting her face. "Mr. Derek sure talks about you a lot."

"Hush," her grandmother said, hiding a smile behind her paper fan. "This child—she never misses a thing and she watches you on the news every night."

"I want to be a reporter when I grow up," Kendra said. "But Granny and Mr. Derek say I have to go to college first."

"That's right," Stephanie said, sitting down in the spot Derek indicated. "Finish school and work hard. That's what I had to do, too."

"I want to be just like you," the little girl replied before her grandmother once again hushed her.

"How sweet." Touched by that declaration and the little girl's endearing smile, Stephanie felt completely humbled. She'd have to remember to send Kendra some goodies from the station. Maybe a T-shirt and plastic cup with the WNT logo on them.

The service started then and Stephanie was left to wonder how Kendra had wound up in a wheelchair. Her life must surely be a struggle, but the kid had spunk. She'd make a fine reporter one day, if she had the right opportunities. Stephanie hoped Kendra could accomplish her dream.

"Thanks for coming," Derek whispered as the minister and choir entered the sanctuary.

Stephanie nodded, then whispered back, "And where are your two wards?" She hadn't seen either Marco or Nathan in the pews.

"Up there," Derek said, motioning toward the front of the church.

Stephanie almost laughed out loud. There amidst the small, multicultural choir stood the two young men she'd seen beating up Walter Griffin. Marco and Nathan were wearing red choir robes, and although they looked uncomfortable at first, when the music started they both got into the rhythm and sang, still with attitude, but with lifted voices all the same.

"'Amazing Grace,'" Stephanie whispered, sure

the choir director had chosen that particular hymn for a very good reason. "You're good, Mr. Kane. Very good. You pull out all the stops."

"I'm determined to save these two from themselves and the neighborhood they grew up in," Derek whispered, his expression so sincere, so secure that Stephanie had no doubt he'd do just that.

More hero material, more fodder for her overly imaginative mind. She had to get to the bottom of this man's story, one way or another. For herself.

Because, she realized as she sat there singing "Amazing Grace," she was fast falling for Derek Kane.

Hero or not.

"We're not used to having a celebrity visit our church," Reverend Byrd told Stephanie after the service. "I hope you'll come back again, though."

Stephanie looked toward where Derek stood underneath a great oak tree down in the yard talking with Marco and Nathan, thinking that very much depended on him. Then she smiled at Reverend Byrd. "I'd like that. And I enjoyed your sermon."

"My brother's keeper," replied the reverend, a tall, lanky red-haired man, his gaze moving over Marco and Nathan. "Sometimes we tend to forget that we are all a part of the family of God."

Stephanie shook his hand and moved on down the receiving line, her mind on Derek. He was now waiting with the boys at the bottom of the steps, with Louise and Kendra by his side. Derek *was* his brother's keeper. The man seemed to do everything right. He rescued damsels in distress, then took villains and tried to turn them into good guys. He helped little old ladies and children in wheelchairs. And he did it all with a quiet dignity.

Or a quiet desperation.

Was Derek trying to atone for some past sin?

Was that why he refused to take any credit or have his actions acknowledged in any way?

"You sure look deep in thought," he said close to her ear as she reached the last of the wooden steps. "Did the reverend's words get to you?"

"In a way, yes," she replied, forcing a smile. "He's right, you know. It's up to us to help out our fellow human beings. I haven't always done the best I could at that job, though."

"You do that every day," Derek pointed out as he steered Kendra's wheelchair toward a waiting van. "You fight the good fight with your stories and your convictions. You've exposed a lot of criminals, brought about changes in politics, opened our eyes to many possibilities—did I leave anything out?"

"Justice is served," she said, a wry smile on her face, not sure why she felt so empty and lacking, in spite of his kind words. "Do you sometimes feel as if we're fighting a losing battle, trying to save the world?"

"Do you feel that way?" he countered, a real concern cresting in his gray eyes.

She shook her head. "I guess I'm just feeling defeated." Nodding toward Marco and Nathan, she added, "Compared to the task you've taken on for the summer, I don't feel nearly so adequate."

Derek stopped her with a hand on her arm. "Hey, don't say that. Don't ever compare what you do to what you *think* I've done. I told you, I'm nobody." He pointed toward the boys, who now stood waiting by his car, Lazarus at their side. "I'm no better, really, than those two I'm trying to help."

"Why would you say that?" she asked, her breath stopping in her throat at the harshness of his words.

Derek looked down at Kendra. The child was laughing and waving to some friends leaving church. He stood there for a long time, just watching the child, the expression on his face torn with torment.

Finally he looked back up at Stephanie. "Just trust me on this, okay? We all have our burdens to bear and I'm no better than the next guy. I'm just trying to make it, one day at a time."

Frustrated at all the walls he insisted on keeping between them, Stephanie could only stare back at him, seeing the hurt, the pain in his haunted eyes.

Derek turned away then, busying himself with lifting Kendra into the van and putting away her wheelchair.

Then Stephanie felt a gentle hand on her arm. Louise Thomas smiled over at her. "I'm glad you came, honey. Derek could use a good friend, someone to talk to now and then, have some fun with. And the way he talks about you, I think he might be headed for even more than just friendship."

Stephanie's heart soared with a bittersweet hope. Miss Nadine had told her much the same thing. Suddenly she realized that Derek had several angels watching over him, making sure he was taken care of, nurtured, loved. Apparently these people hadn't given up on him. They thought he was worth fighting for.

And so did Stephanie.

Knowing this, acknowledging her own growing feelings for him, made him even more appealing, more endearing in her eyes.

"Thank you," she said to Louise, unable to convey her true feelings. She had so many questions to ask the woman, but they all died on her lips. "I hope to see you again sometime."

"I'm sure you will," Louise replied, her tone and expression as steady and sure as the sun and the wind.

The next few weeks passed by in that same sure and steady pace for Stephanie. Glover had been assigned a major story centered on an important vote at the next city council meeting, so he didn't have time to hover around asking questions about Derek. And her own work kept her occupied enough that she wasn't tempted to dig through more records to search for the missing link on Derek. After all, she knew everything there was to know about the man. Everything that mattered.

And yet, her heart had many questions. Her heart pondered and wondered and worried. Derek was nursing a great wound, a wound that went deep and bothered him often. She still remembered that look of torment he'd had on his face as he stood staring down at little Kendra.

She now believed that while he hadn't done anything criminal, he was blaming himself for something that had happened—maybe a love affair gone bad, or a relationship or job that had left him devastated. And she also knew if she pushed, she could find out anything she wanted to know. There were so many ways to get information on people—it was ridiculously easy, especially for a reporter.

And yet, she'd stopped, deliberately holding back. Because of her own fear, because of her promise to Derek to let the matter die, because the more she longed to know, the more she convinced herself that she didn't really care anymore.

Now she cared more about the man he was today. Now she wanted only to move forward, and let the past rest. So she struggled, waffling between getting to the truth and getting to know the man. Her goal now was for Derek to open up and tell her about his past, to trust her as a friend, and maybe…even more.

And apparently he felt the same way about her. They were seeing each other on a regular basis.

But when Stephanie was with him, which was more and more often, he was funny, caring, interesting and still a mystery.

They spent time at the lake, taking boat rides in his small motorboat, or better yet, sailing together in his larger sailboat, Lazarus ever faithful by his master's side. Sometimes Marco and Nathan joined them, always watchful and full of attitude, but ever mindful that Derek and Lazarus were in charge of the situation.

Last night, however, the boys had been assigned to shore duty. Derek had had them scrubbing and weatherproofing the dock. When Stephanie had expressed worry that the boys would slip away, Derek had explained this was their first test. They were trying out the honor system. And, he'd said with a wry grin, he had a backup plan. Reverend Byrd and a couple of deacons from the church would be fishing off the nearby bank, with one eye turned toward their young wards.

So Stephanie and Derek had had some precious time alone on the sailboat, except for Lazarus. Even the dog had gotten a reprieve from his duties. As they'd sailed close to the shore on the wings of a breathtaking sunset, Stephanie had asked Derek about his dog, and later about Kendra and her grandmother.

"How long have you had Lazarus?"

Once again Derek had seemed hesitant, unsure how much he should tell her. "Since he was about a year old—five years now."

"Did you get him at the humane society?"

"No. From a friend."

And that had been it. No explanations, no funny stories of chewed-up shoes or puppy training mishaps.

"Did you train him yourself?" she'd asked a few minutes later.

"I had some help. He's trained as a watchdog, but he's really just a big softie."

Okay. Stephanie had sat silent for a while, then asked, "How did you meet Louise? She's such a nice lady. And little Kendra is a doll."

"Yeah, they're both special to me."

Not a complete answer. Not nearly a complete answer.

Somehow, after that, Derek had managed to turn the conversation away from himself, just as he always did. And he'd also managed to quiet her inquiring mind in the only way they both could agree on.

He'd kissed her.

Long and tenderly, and with a longing that left her only wanting more.

"Are you trying to get rid of me?" she'd teased on a whisper of breath.

"Nah, not this time. You're kinda growing on me. And besides, I couldn't do that to Laz again. That poor dog's got a big crush on you."

At the mention of his name, the animal had given a halfhearted bark, then rolled over amid rigging and life preservers at Stephanie's feet, his doleful eyes begging her to pay attention to him.

So there they'd sat on the sailboat, the three of them, man, woman and dog, watching the gold-and-pink sunset flirt with the tree line, watching the moon rise on a brilliant cloudless dusk.

Stephanie had never felt so close to Derek—his kisses anchored her and held her, making her feel warm and safe, secure, and yet this morning she felt as if she were out on that lake again, drifting, unsure, lost in uncharted waters.

"Maybe it's time to go visit my mother," she said to herself as she shifted through files and tapped out copy on the computer screen. If she got caught up by week's end, she'd do just that. Take a nice long drive up to the mountains, to clear her head, to listen to her heart. "That's exactly what I need."

"You sure do talk to yourself a lot," Glover said from behind her, making her jump.

"Do you have to sneak up on me like that all the time?" Stephanie said on a huff. "Honestly, Glover, you must have special sneakers made just for you, so you can surprise all your sources.''

''I am a reporter,'' he pointed out as he plopped down in a nearby chair. ''And I learned from the best.''

Stephanie saw his nod toward her, then smiled. ''We've been through some tough assignments together, haven't we?''

He leaned forward then, his brown eyes assessing her with a steady, disquieting calm. ''Yes, we have. We've been competitive, but when push comes to shove, we make a good team, working together.''

She noticed the way he emphasized the working together part. Lately, they hadn't had much opportunity for teamwork. Stephanie had surpassed her buddy, and was receiving more and more attention and perks for her hard work. But Glover worked just as hard, even if she didn't always agree with his tactics.

Hoping to show him that she still supported him, she tapped her pen on a file. ''What are you working on?''

''Not much,'' he said, sighing before he crossed his arms and leaned back against the padded chair. ''We wrapped up the report on the city council. The vote passed in spite of the opposition. Since then, it's been a slow week. No blood or fire.'' He glanced at her blinking screen. ''Besides, we both know who gets the plum assignments these days. The ratings say everything, don't they?"

"Our ratings are always high," she replied, uncomfortable with the tone of this conversation. "Because we work hard—all of us. And that includes you."

"Sure," he said, pushing himself up off the chair. "Speaking of work, guess I better get back to that story of sewage problems over near Grant Park. The zoo board is up in arms, saying it will affect the tourist traffic."

Wrinkling her nose in disgust, Stephanie said, "Well, I guess so. That stinks."

He laughed then, easing some of the tension Stephanie could feel. Then he looked down at her. "Stef, are you still dating Derek Kane?"

Wondering why he wanted to know, Stephanie felt a sense of unease. She wanted to trust Glover, but she knew him so well. And her instincts told her that he was still eager to find out what both she and Derek were hiding. "I see him now and then, nothing serious."

Glover nodded. "So you never followed through on the gardening story?"

"No. It was too soft. Not enough meat. And we're so far into summer now, it's about too late to give gardening tips."

"Yeah. It just surprises me, how you seem to be

so closemouthed about that man. Almost as if you're trying to protect him.''

Meeting his questioning gaze head-on, Stephanie stood up. ''I am protecting him, Glover. I'm dating the man, not doing an exposé on him. And because it's personal, I think Derek and I have a right to some privacy. I don't see why you think there's a story there.''

He shrugged. ''Maybe because even Claire has told me to leave it alone. Maybe because you're trying so hard to keep me away from the man.'' Pushing at his rolled-up shirtsleeves, he grinned. ''Just kinda makes a fellow wonder, you know?''

Irritated, and more than worried, Stephanie pushed past him. ''Well, stop worrying. Don't lose any sleep over Derek Kane. I'm certainly not.''

She'd just told a whopper of a white lie. She'd lost more sleep over Derek Kane than she cared to think about.

And from the dubious expression on James Glover's face, she could tell he knew that she wasn't being honest. He also knew that she was trying desperately to shield Derek.

She'd have to either warn Derek, or pick back up where she'd left off with her own private investigation, both of which she'd been trying hard to avoid.

If she didn't find out everything there was to

know about Derek's past, and soon, James would beat her to the punch and...he really wouldn't lose any sleep over it.

Then Derek would never forgive her.

Chapter Eleven

Stephanie put her hands on her hips and stared at the group of people clustered in Derek's backyard. "When you invited me for a cookout, I didn't realize we'd be entertaining the whole town."

Derek flipped another burger, then called out over his shoulder to Stephanie, "Oh, did you want to be alone with me? 'Cause that can be arranged, if you insist."

Stephanie grinned as she glanced around. The eclectic group included the ever-present Marco and Nathan, who were in charge of the volleyball game, Lazarus, who was in charge of Marco and Nathan—the dog was secretly having a blast just playing with the two—Louise Thomas and Kendra, Reverend Byrd and his wife and five children, and much to everyone's surprise, a special guest of honor, Miss Nadine Hamilton, of the Atlanta Hamiltons.

Tugging at the Atlanta Braves baseball cap Derek wore, Stephanie laughed. "Sure, I suppose you can make all of these relaxed, laid-back people scatter just by telling them that you'd like to kiss me in private?"

"Yes, ma'am," he said, winking over at her. "And please don't tempt me like that."

"Let's keep our guests happy and let them stay," she said, munching on a pickle slice. "Besides, I'm starving. I can't wait to try one of your famous burgers, since you've bragged about them all afternoon."

He grinned again. "It ain't bragging if it's true."

"Now who's doing the tempting?" she teased back.

He checked the long row of sizzling meat, then let out an elaborate sigh. "Let's see, you prefer burgers and a crowd over being alone with me. I just can't seem to take this relationship any further."

"Do you want to take things further?" she asked, her tone turning serious, her words for his ears only.

"You should know the answer to that," he responded, his gaze on her instead of his precious burgers.

"No, I don't know," she had to admit. "We've been together almost every weekend and several week nights after work for the last couple of weeks, Derek, but—"

"But you still want some answers?" He looked up at her, his gray eyes filling with those storm clouds she was beginning to recognize and understand.

"Yes," she said finally, "but not for the reasons you think. I want to know you, Derek, to understand you, to see a picture of you from beginning to end. I want to meet your big family and hear stories about you in grammar school, and I want to take all that information and process it, so I can have a complete picture of the man I'm—"

He dropped the spatula then, turning to touch a hand to each of her bare arms. "Falling for?" he finished, hope as bright in his eyes as the sun reflecting off the water.

"Yes," she said, glad to get that little tidbit out of the way. "Derek, we need to talk, really talk. I want to help you—"

Just then, Marco called for Derek. "Hey, man, we need you on our team. Miss Nadine's pretty good with that serve."

Derek had to laugh then, as both he and Stephanie turned to watch spry Miss Nadine take a dainty fist to the big ball and lob it right over the net, then step back with a prim smile to straighten her navy cotton flared skirt. Two of the Byrd children, who happened to be Miss Nadine's teammates, cheered loudly as another point was scored.

"Who knew?" Derek said, taking Stephanie by

the hand. "Guess we'd better go even out the game."

"Derek?" Stephanie held back.

He stopped, took another deep breath.

During that brief second or two, she could see the struggle there on his tanned face and in his stormy eyes.

"Derek, I have to know, for me. Only for me."

And to protect you, she wanted to say. Glover had been snooping all week, asking questions, prying way beyond measure. Stephanie's gut instinct told her the other reporter wouldn't give up. And the more James Glover pushed, the more determined Stephanie was to protect Derek, and let *him* tell her his story. She badly wanted to earn his trust, so she wouldn't have to stoop to investigating him on her own.

"We will talk," he said finally. "Today, after everyone goes home. I'll tell you everything, Stephanie. And then we'll see if you still think you might be falling for me."

A few minutes later she fell straight into his arms in a heated volleyball game where Miss Nadine stood and served, then stepped back and watched as the "take no prisoners" competitors went after the ball.

When both Derek and Stephanie rushed to return the serve, they got the ball over the net, then crashed into each other. Derek fell first, then cushioned Stephanie's fall. In a tangle of legs and arms, they lay laughing and panting for breath while everyone around them clapped.

"Nice save," she said as she gazed down at him. It took all of her willpower not to reach out and touch his scarred, intriguing face. Especially when she knew these scars ran much deeper than he ever wanted to admit.

Derek stared up at her, a look of tenderness in his dark eyes. And a lot of unspoken promises. "We'd better get up, or people will talk."

With that, he lifted her up with a strong hand, then bowed as Nathan and Marco high-fived each other. While the boys protested, Derek gestured toward the grill. "Duty calls, fellows."

When they got out of earshot of the others, Stephanie leaned close. "Derek, it's amazing what you've done with those two in just a couple of weeks," she said, proud in spite of her earlier reservations about Derek taking on the two boys.

He shrugged. "They mainly needed some guidance. Marco is the oldest of eight children. They live in a house no bigger than my storage shed. His mom tries to work to support them, but with all those kids and no father figure, it's tough. Marco met up with Nathan, and was headed toward a career selling drugs for the gang leaders. He'd already had a few run-ins with the police, but this last bit scared his mother. She was very grateful to the judge for allowing him into this intervention program."

He glanced over at the boys, who were now resting and talking with Reverend Byrd. "And Nathan—his mother left long ago and his father was killed in a brawl. He lives with his uncle, and from what I've seen that man is not much of a role model. Nathan's way of solving problems is to fight first and ask questions later."

Amazed that Derek, a single man who could be off sailing on the lake right now, had taken the time to help these troubled boys, Stephanie asked, "Have you done this before?"

He shrugged again, his attention on taking up the food. "It's a program that was started at an inner-city church in downtown Atlanta. When I moved to Flowery Branch and met Reverend Byrd, he told me about it. I guess he thought it might help me—getting involved with other people." He stopped, his gaze rising out over the lake. "Anyway, it's called Justice Through Faith. Basically, the local churches work with the police and the juvenile justice system to try and intervene and help reform troubled kids."

"I'd sure love to do a story on this," Stephanie said, then seeing the wary look in his eyes, hastily added, "Someday, whenever you're ready. Or with Reverend Byrd at the center. People need to know more about this."

"I can't argue with that."

She smiled as she helped him finish getting the food ready, while Miss Nadine went from volleyball captain to social director, issuing orders on proper picnic etiquette.

"Justice Through Faith," Stephanie said, yet again amazed, and once more feeling that tug of familiarity. "I have a framed Bible quote on my desk that my mother gave to me after my father's death. 'The just shall live by faith.' I guess I never thought we can save people from a life of crime by concentrating first on their faith. But my father knew that. And so do you, it seems." And maybe that was the only reason his actions seemed so familiar.

Derek finished his work, then turned to her. "Stephanie, you're a Christian. You know the power of Jesus Christ, right?"

"I do," she said. Then she lowered her head. "But I haven't always used that power. I'm too stubborn, too independent. It's hard to rely on something you can't see or explain away in a carefully researched story."

Derek took her hands in his, his whole expression tender, his eyes centered only on her. "I couldn't have survived…without God and Jesus in my life. And I know that if I fight hard for these boys, with the Lord on my side I can make a difference. Instead of carting them off to a place where they slip into a further abyss, I can give them hope and a new life, just like the Lord gave us."

Tears pricked Stephanie's eyes. "God did send you to me that night, Derek. And whether you want to admit it or not, you are a good and decent man. I'm not so sure I deserve you, though."

"Don't say that," he told her, reaching up to wipe away a tear. "I'm the one who doesn't deserve any of this, but for some reason, the good Lord has given me a second chance. I'm hoping that chance includes you, Stephanie."

Smiling up at him then, in spite of the threatening tears, she said in a droll voice, "Well, maybe He put us together because we can't seem to feel worthy apart—maybe He has a sense of humor, putting two such unworthy souls with each other."

"But together, who knows? We might find redemption after all."

Derek hugged her close, and Stephanie felt the urgency of that hug. She was winning his trust; she could feel it, see it in the way he had grown more intimate with her. And later, maybe he would at last tell her everything she longed to hear.

"Excuse me," Miss Nadine said from behind them. "If you two don't mind, we have guests to feed."

In spite of her stern tone, Stephanie saw the delighted twinkle in the older woman's eyes.

Louise pushed Kendra's wheelchair close. Miss Nadine bent down to talk to the child. "I'm so glad

I finally got to meet you, Kendra. Your grandmother and Mr. Kane are both very proud of you."

"Thank you," Kendra said, beaming. "Mr. Derek takes good care of us."

Stephanie didn't miss the wealth of information in that innocent statement, or the way, upon hearing the girl's words, Derek's eyes clouded over with doubt and that old haunted look she'd seen when they first met. Why did Derek feel obligated to watch over Kendra and her grandmother? Was it duty and affection, or something more?

Hoping she'd find out the answers to that particular puzzle later, she decided to concentrate on being with Derek and his many friends right now.

Breaking away from Derek, she called out. "Okay, who wants a famous Derek Kane hamburger?"

Nathan and Marco were first in line, but Reverend Byrd halted them. "Shall we say grace?"

Everyone bowed their heads while the reverend blessed the food and thanked Derek for inviting all of them. "May God's grace continue to shine on this group, and may His love carry all of us through the uncertain waters of life."

"Amen," came the chorus before everyone scrambled for the serving table.

"You know, man, you're all right," Marco said to Derek, his expression just this side of cool. Then he looked out over the sparkling water. "I kinda wish I could stay here forever, Mr. Derek."

Derek lifted his chin a notch. "Me, too, buddy."

"Do you feel safe here?" Stephanie asked as she got in line behind the tall youth.

Marco eyed her suspiciously, then shrugged. "I like it here. It's peaceful and there's lots to do. But I miss my brothers and sisters. And I'm worried—I don't want 'em to get hurt."

"Do you think someone might retaliate, try to get even with you through them?" Stephanie asked.

Marco rolled his eyes, then took on the tough-guy stance she'd seen the night of the mugging. "Lady, don't you understand? Getting even is the name of the game where I come from."

Stephanie could hear the bitterness in his words, but before she could respond, he continued. "*Miss* Maguire—" Derek had told them to address her as such, and so far they had respected that firm request "—you could help out, you know. You could do a story on our neighborhood. It's bad there, real bad, and me and Nathan were right in the thick of it."

"Do you want to go back?" Stephanie asked.

Nathan stepped forward then, balancing a plate loaded with food. "Not really, but hey, we can't all have a place on a lake, can we?" He gave Derek a sarcastic look.

"Son, do you know how hard Mr. Kane worked for this spot on the lake?" Miss Nadine asked, her fingers apparently itching to take Nathan by the ear and shake him.

Nathan shrugged. "All I know is, he makes us work day and night, and I'm getting mighty tired of it. We don't get to watch television or listen to music. He won't even let us play a video game."

"Would you rather be in juvenile jail?" Miss Nadine asked in a sweet tone, as if she were asking the kid if he'd like more sugar with his tea.

Nathan scowled, shrugged again, then moved off to eat his food, Marco trailing along behind him.

"We're still working on that one," Derek told Stephanie. "He's a real challenge. Tough as nails and determined to hold out to the bitter end."

"Marco seems to be coming around," Stephanie said. "He's really got a sweet streak, and he seems genuinely worried about his family. He's so different from the person I saw beating up Mr. Griffin that night."

"Yes, if we can just nurture his good side and win him over, he might be redeemable. But Nathan—I'm worried about him. I have to watch him day and night. He likes to snoop and plunder, probably because he's been trained to steal. He doesn't have the same respect for other people's property as Marco."

Stephanie watched as the two boys ate their meal. Maybe Marco was right. Maybe she should stop worrying about investigating Derek and concentrate on getting to the bottom of the situation that had forced these two to come close to a life of crime.

Sighing, she realized she'd been neglecting her work a lot lately. Before she'd met Derek, her work was all she had. So she'd poured her heart into it. It was rewarding, but now she could see that there was so much more to life. And because of him, she'd been taking more time to relax, all because she hoped to get to know him better. But she still had obligations, as Claire reminded her every day. Even her producer, who usually was her biggest ally, had complained that Stephanie hadn't brought in any hard-hitting news in the past couple of weeks.

After tonight, she told herself as she nibbled on her food. *Once Derek and I sit down and talk, and he tells me everything, then I can get back to concentrating on my job.*

And maybe then she could waylay James Glover and tell him he really didn't need to continue pestering her about Derek. Maybe Derek's past wasn't newsworthy, but Stephanie needed to know about it. And James needed to back off.

He'd probably laugh when he told him that Derek had led a normal life, growing up in the country. No story. No need to keep digging.

She glanced over at Derek, saw the worry on his face and wondered all over again if she'd be able to deal with what he had to tell her.

* * *

Derek finished putting trash into the huge can located near the table. Everyone had gone home except Stephanie. She insisted on helping to clean up.

"I had fun today," she told him now as she dropped some paper cups into the open container. "Miss Nadine had a good time, too, I think."

"I can't believe she actually came," Derek replied, enjoying the way the late-afternoon sun played across Stephanie's dark hair. "She's taken a keen interest in my two roommates, though. Says she's out to save their wretched souls."

"Then she sits them down to tell them about the salvation of the Lord," Stephanie finished. "And with a smile on her face."

Derek laughed. "I think I saw them reading the Bible together earlier."

Stephanie nodded. "And I think those two have found a friend in Miss Nadine Hamilton. Her faith is so strong, how can Marco and Nathan not be moved?"

"I'm worried about Nathan. He seems determined to just get through this so he can get back to doing exactly what he was doing before," Derek said, checking to make sure the two were in his sight.

Stephanie glanced over at the boys. Derek had them sweeping up trash and putting away lawn chairs. Nathan had a perpetual scowl centered on his tanned face, while Marco seemed uncertain what to do next. "It's going to be a long summer," she said to Derek.

Derek watched her, still amazed that she'd told him she might be falling for him. Ever since he'd found out that her father had been a lawman, Derek had worried about his own growing feelings for Stephanie. How would she react to the news that he was an ex-cop? He'd wanted to tell her, had tried to bring himself to let her know. But then he'd have to explain everything, and he just wasn't ready for that.

At least she didn't have to worry about his current occupation. It was as tame as any job could be.

Better than him being a cop, he guessed. He hoped. But being an ex-cop was one thing. Being an ex-cop with an ugly past was another. He'd decided to level with her, because he cared about her. Now he was afraid telling her the truth would scare her away.

Funny, he'd wanted to scare her off in the beginning. Now he only wanted to hold her near and protect her, shield her from the harsh reality of his past. And he appreciated the way she'd backed down. He believed her when she said she wasn't investigating him anymore, except for personal reasons. Maybe it was time to be honest with Stephanie.

No sense in putting it off. He'd leave the matter in God's hands and hope that Stephanie would understand.

If not, well…he'd been alone before.

Turning to Marco and Nathan, Derek called out. "Hey, you two, go in the garage and get a couple more trash bags. We might as well finish up and take this trash out to the road."

Marco nodded, then headed for the big garage that was off to the side of the main house. Nathan followed close on his heels. With a silent command, Derek instructed Lazarus to stay close to the boys.

"You want to trust them, don't you?" Stephanie asked now, her gaze falling across Derek like a warm wind.

"I have to trust them, in order to win their trust," he explained. "And I hope I can do the same thing with you."

"I trust you," she said, the honesty of the statement taking his breath away. "I always have."

"But I haven't always felt the same," he admitted, taking her by the hand. "Stephanie, I've got so much to say, and I don't know how to begin."

"How about at the beginning," she said. "Derek, I could have found out everything I wanted to know and then some about you, weeks ago. You realize that, don't you?"

He nodded. "I know. And I've wondered just how much you have found out on your own."

"I stopped trying," she said, the sincerity on her face making him believe her. "But I haven't stopped wondering."

She reached up to touch a tiny scar on his left cheek. "I wonder about your wounds, Derek. Not just the surface wounds, but the wounds deep inside you. Here." She touched her hand to his heart. "I want to help you to heal."

Derek wrapped his hand over hers, then brought it to his lips for a brief kiss. Closing his eyes, he moved her hand to his cheek, to the scar she'd touched earlier. "I don't know if you can help me."

He stood there, silent, holding her to him. And he prayed for strength, for peace, for forgiveness. He didn't want to lose this woman.

"Derek?"

He opened his eyes to find her watching him, a look of tenderness centered in her big eyes.

"Trust me," she said, her finger tracing a soft, warm pattern over the scar. "Please?"

He nodded, lifted his head toward hers.

And then Nathan burst out of the garage, a look of complete rage causing his face to redden as he went for Derek. "You tricked us, man. You brought us here, making us think you really cared. But you didn't bother telling us that you're a cop!"

Chapter Twelve

Stephanie felt the blood rushing to her head as everything became a blur of motion then. Nathan dropped the box he was carrying, then pushed Derek to the ground before pouncing on top of him.

Marco came running out of the garage, a look of fear on his dark features as he tried to pick up the scattered things that had fallen out of the box.

Lazarus, thinking Nathan was attacking his master, started barking and snarling at the boy. With a quick shouted command, Derek stopped the dog from jumping on Nathan, then managed to roll and hold Nathan down himself.

"Listen to me," Derek said, his teeth gritted, his breath coming hard and fast as he held the boy's flailing arms. "You've got it all wrong."

He glanced up at Stephanie, but she was already

backing away. Finding a nearby lawn chair, she sank into it, then dropped her head in her hands, unable to watch while Derek yanked Nathan up and pushed him away. When she looked back up, Derek was kneeling at her side.

"I can explain," he said, his voice shaky from exertion, his expression a mixture of anger and shame.

She saw Marco and Nathan scowling down at them, Lazarus still snarling at the two shocked boys.

"Sit down," Derek told the boys. When they only glared at him, he shouted, "I said sit down!"

They both found chairs a few feet away, amid the scattered pictures and official-looking papers that had fallen out of the storage box, along with a coffee cup that had an emblem emblazoned across its surface.

Stephanie knew the mug had properly been given to Derek through a police department somewhere. Her father had had one very similar to it.

"It all makes perfect sense now," she said, her gaze flying from the boys back to Derek. "I knew. I just knew. There was something so familiar about you—your actions, your whole stance, your whole demeanor. I thought you just reminded me of my father. I thought I was imagining things. But it's true. You're a cop. You walk like one, act like one—it's so obvious in every step you take, in every little action, the alert way you scope out a room when you walk into it, or the way you question people, even the way you stare at strangers.'' She looked up, tears rolling down her cheeks. "You're a cop, Derek. Why didn't you tell me? Or better yet, why didn't I just admit it to myself?''

Nathan jumped up then. "I'll tell you all about him!'' He lifted a pile of papers from the box. "I found pictures—a whole book of pictures. *Him* graduating from the academy. *Him* with his gun—a Glock semiautomatic, man, standard issue. Do you have that gun hidden somewhere in your house? *Him* getting all kinds of medals and promotions.''

He pointed to his chest. "What'd this little piece of undercover work get you, huh? Were you hoping to win me and Marco here over, to get inside the gang, break it up, by pretending to be our friend, our *mentor,* by pretending to be some holy roller who'd save our souls?''

The look of disgust and betrayal on Nathan's face told the tale in a long, deafening silence. And so did the look of anguish on Derek's face.

He sank down on the ground, one hand on Stephanie's arm, then looked up at the boys. "I need you two to sit there and listen,'' he said, the words more of a plea than a command.

Lazarus seemed to understand, even if the humans didn't. The dog sat down right at the boys' feet, his dark eyes daring either of them to make a move.

Stephanie waited, her heart pounding, breaking.

Derek couldn't be a cop. He would have at least told her the truth about that. She'd asked him if he was working undercover and he'd denied it, but from the look on his face now, what Nathan was saying was true.

Finally Derek let her go to stand up. "I *was* a police officer," he said, his voice edged with a bone-weary tiredness. "I *was,* a few years ago." Then he looked down at Stephanie. "But I'm retired now. And you don't have to worry. I had to turn my gun and my badge back in. I'll never be a cop again."

She saw the look of torment in his eyes. She saw the pain centered there, like a rising cloud swirling out over deep waters. Whatever had happened, it had done this to him. It had caused him to shut himself off from the world, from everything and everyone. It had caused him to leave his former life behind, to hide from the world, to start a new identity. He'd been safe here in his little world. Until now.

"Why didn't you tell me?" she asked, crushed that he'd let her go on and on about her father, hurt that he hadn't even trusted her enough to explain about his past.

"I couldn't," he said, his voice raspy, the words almost in a whisper. "Because then I'd have to tell you why I'm no longer an officer of the law."

She jumped up to face him. "So this is what

you've been hiding. This is why the Atlanta police department protected you and shielded you. That wall of blue held the truth from me. Why didn't they want me to know? Why didn't you want me to know, Derek? What did you do that was so terrible?''

"It didn't happen here in Atlanta," he said, pushing a hand through his hair. "I worked for a small town down in Florida. Just a few officers."

"But that gave you connections here?"

"Yes. That's one of the reasons I moved here. A friend suggested it. That and…other reasons."

"And are you ready to tell me about those other reasons?"

He searched her face, then turned to Nathan and Marco. "I can't right now. I can't. I wanted to, but I can see now that would be a mistake all the way around. I wish I hadn't encouraged you, Stephanie. I should have gone with my gut instinct and stayed away from you, but it's too late now."

"Derek?"

He held up a hand. "No, you'd better just leave, Stephanie. Go! I mean it. Leave right now, before we have any more regrets, before this situation gets even worse. Okay?"

"I can't," she said, reaching out to him. "I have to know the truth. And you have to trust me."

"I don't think—" He stopped, pushed her away. "Just go."

The boys, now quiet and watchful, sent secretive looks toward each other.

"He won't tell us," Nathan said, his tone accusing. "Cops don't ever have to answer to anybody."

"Hush," Marco retorted, slapping his friend on the arm. "Can't you see—the man didn't do a thing to us. This is all in the past. He's trying to help us."

"Once a cop, always a cop, in my mind," Nathan replied, but he quieted down, then hung his head. "I sure thought you were different, man."

Derek's face was a study in anguish. He looked away, out over the dusk-kissed trees. "I wish I could explain—"

"Derek, please?" Stephanie moved toward him, wanting to understand, wanting to comfort him. "Can't you trust me enough to tell me the truth? Don't you owe these boys that much, at least? Or would you rather I just leave and let you explain things to them?"

He backed away, holding up a hand toward her. "Don't do this. I told you when we first met that I didn't want any publicity or recognition. I tried to warn you."

Stephanie refused to back down. "But *I* told you all about my father. And you just sat there, never once letting me in on your little secret." She stopped, remembering the night she'd poured her soul out to him, remembering the way he'd reacted. "That's why you clammed up again. That's why you seemed so quiet that night. You didn't tell me then and you probably were never going to tell me. Do you know how much that hurts, Derek?''

"Yes, I know," he said, his words coming in a harsh snarl. "How could I tell you something like that, when you've had to live with your father's death all this time? How could I explain, Stephanie? Oh, I'm sorry about your father and by the way, I used to be a cop myself? I didn't want to add to your pain. I didn't want you to know, and not just for my own selfish reasons—I was trying to protect you."

"I don't need protection," she said. "I need the truth."

"Well, you won't get it from me."

"Then I'll find out on my own, which is what I should have done to begin with. I almost kept at it, but because I cared about you and respected your wishes, I stalled out. I gave up, hoping you'd be honest with me, hoping *you'd* give me the answers I needed."

And all this time, I've had to keep my eye on Glover, to fight against going on with my investigation. But she couldn't tell Derek that. Not now.

Her mind full of a red haze of humiliation and rage, she turned to grab her purse. She had to get away from him. She had to think, to work through this, to dig and dig until she found out everything he seemed so determined to keep from her.

Looking down, she stumbled on one of the pictures Nathan had found. Derek stood by a patrol car, smiling, wearing a blue uniform. How could she not have seen this? Maybe because she'd blocked it. Maybe because she hadn't wanted to know the truth. She'd wanted a hero. A perfect hero. So she'd denied her need to see reality. She'd even denied doing her job, which was to always, always get the story. Well, no more.

Reaching down to scoop up the photo, she stuffed it in her straw purse. She didn't dare look back.

Even as Stephanie walked away, she could *feel* him following her. Without turning around, she said, "Don't try to stop me, Derek."

He held a hand to her car door, forcing her to look up at him. "I'm not going to stop you. But I am going to ask you to stay away from me. Don't come back here, Stephanie."

She whirled to glare up at him, her eyes brimming. "Even if I do find the truth, even if I don't care what horrible things you did in your past?" She swallowed back the tears burning her throat. "Even if I love you, Derek?"

He stared at her as if he couldn't quite believe what she'd just said, his eyes misty with unspoken words, his heart showing through the gray battered stone of his gaze. "Even then," he said.

And then he turned and stalked away, his back straight, his beautiful body rigid with pride.

His whole stance that of a police officer.

The next morning Stephanie arrived at work to find Claire waiting for her.

"I need to see you in my office," the producer said, her half-moon-shaped earrings clinking as she took off in the direction she'd just indicated.

"I have some work—"

"It can wait."

Stephanie followed, physically and emotionally drained. Just what she needed, another lecture on how she'd been slipping up lately. Following Claire into the office, she waited as the other woman shut the door.

Taking off her dark sunglasses, Stephanie faced Claire. "What's up?"

Claire took one look at Stephanie's red-rimmed eyes and sank onto the chair centered behind her cluttered desk. "Kid, you look downright rough. Cry yourself to sleep last night, or did you suffer through one of those horrible headaches again?"

"A little of both," Stephanie admitted. "But it won't affect my work."

"I think you have bigger problems," Claire replied.

"Nothing I can't handle," Stephanie said, determination making her jaw clench. "Just go ahead and tell me what I need to do. I'm planning on working late tonight, anyway."

"Oh, no." Claire leaned back in her chair, her gaze moving over Stephanie's face. "First I think you need to tell me just how involved you've become with Derek Kane. I mean, that is what this is all about, isn't it?"

Stephanie wasn't in the mood to divulge everything that had happened with Derek. "Let's just stick to work, okay, Claire? I can deal with my personal life on my own."

"Are you sure?" Claire asked, taking a sip of the herbal tea she kept handy. "I did call you in here to talk about that, Stef—both your personal life and your work. You seem to be spending more time with Mr. Kane and less time tracking down newsworthy stories. Lately I've been worried about you."

"I've completed all my assignments, and I'm working on two different stories right now," Stephanie retorted. "Have I ever let you down before, Claire?"

"No, of course not. But I can worry about you, can't I? It just seems you've spent the last few weeks obsessing over Derek Kane. You've lost some of your drive, some of your pep, and you have yet to tell me the whole story."

"There is no story!" Stephanie jumped up to pace around the cluttered office. "Why can't you and James just back off and let me have a personal life for a change? You'd think I don't have a right to date anyone without it becoming a major issue around here.''

"Hey, hey.'' Claire came around the desk then to lay a hand across Stephanie's back. "Just calm down. You've had a lot of relationships since I've known you, but I've never seen you like this before. You were the one determined to go after Derek's story. You had this hunch, right? Well, it backfired on you, kid. You've gone and fallen in love with the man and we still don't know a thing about his past.''

"I know enough,'' Stephanie said, ashamed at how she'd lashed out at Claire. Quieter now, she added, "I know more now than I did a few days ago.''

"Oh, really?''

"Yes. He's an ex-cop, Claire.''

Claire placed a well-manicured fingernail to her chin. Her face twisted in a grimace. "That changes things, doesn't it?''

Stephanie crossed her arms over her midsection. "Not really. Except that things are over between Derek and me. He told me to leave him alone.''

"Because you found out he once was a cop?''

"Yes.''

"But that makes it even more interesting. Why does he want you to leave him alone, unless he's hiding something?''

Stephanie pushed a hand through the hair trailing

around her face. "Because apparently he's still having trouble dealing with whatever happened back then." She stopped, looked out the window where a spectacular view of the Atlanta skyline beckoned her. "I saw something there in his eyes last night...when he told me to never come back."

"What did you see, honey?"

"He loves me." She turned to face Claire again. "He loves me, but he doesn't think he deserves anybody's love."

"You're sure of this."

Stephanie shrugged. "No. Right now I can't be sure of anything, but I *felt* it. He's pushing me away deliberately. And I have to find out why."

Claire patted her on the arm. "You're way too involved in this, kid. Why don't you let Glover help you out? He can have a more objective point of view about our Mr. Kane."

"No." Stephanie walked toward the door. "I don't want Glover anywhere near Derek. That would just destroy all the trust I've worked so hard to build with him."

"But you said he loves you. Shouldn't that make him more willing to trust you?"

"You'd think so, wouldn't you?"

With that, Stephanie left the office and headed down the hallway toward her own cubicle. She spent the rest of the day bogged down in work, trying hard to put Derek out of her mind. She'd never let anything or anyone interfere with her career before, and she wasn't about to let that change now. In spite of the great pain piercing her heart.

Yet temptation won out. When she'd finished editing her story for that night's broadcast, she pulled out the picture of Derek she'd found lying on the ground last night. With a shaking finger she traced his face, his smile, his eyes. He looked happy, proud and very much a lawman.

If she knew Derek Kane the way she thought she did, he'd probably relished being a policeman. He would have been good at his job, the best. So what would make him give it all up and move to an isolated spot on a lake in north Georgia?

Had he been corrupt? Caught up in something beyond his control? Had he been dismissed from his duties, or had he walked away forever on his own terms?

She had to find out.

Turning, she gasped as she saw Glover standing about a foot from her desk, staring down at the picture.

"That's Derek Kane, isn't it?"

On a defeated breath, she nodded. "Yes. I found out last night that he used to be a police officer. And we broke things off. So now will you please leave me alone?"

Glover came closer, his gaze staying on the picture. "Where did he work?"

"Please, Glover. Let it go."

"Stef, you know I can't do that. And you have to admit, you're as curious as I am. What can it hurt to just find out some more information on the man?"

Remembering that Glover still didn't know Derek was the Good Samaritan everyone had been talking about a few weeks ago, she dropped the picture.

"C'mon, Stef. It can't hurt to check things out, right? In our spare time, just to be sure."

I'll hurt, she wanted to tell him. But he was right. This had been her goal, her one desire since the night she'd bumped into Derek. Now was her chance. He'd demanded she stay away from him, but that demand couldn't keep her from finding out the truth.

And once she did, she'd show Derek Kane how wrong he'd been about her. She'd show him that he needed to learn how to trust again.

And, dear Lord, maybe I need to learn that, too.

"Okay, what do you have?"

Stephanie looked across the table at James, waiting for him to wipe the satisfied smirk off his face.

"You won't believe," he said, settling down to take a long drink from the glass of soda the waitress at the secluded suburban restaurant had just brought him.

"Just get on with it, Glover," she said on a sharp

voice. Her nerves felt as if thorns were poking into them, and she was sure she was on the verge of another migraine. And finding out Glover had information on Derek hadn't helped matters.

"I managed to get access to his bank account," Glover said, clearly impressed with himself.

"How? I told you I don't like your tactics."

"Never mind how, and you don't need to know. But your Mr. Kane is making monthly payments to someone named Louise Thomas. Hefty payments. Any reason why he might be doing that?"

Stephanie sank back against her chair. "They're friends. She has a granddaughter who's disabled. Maybe he's just helping them out."

"Maybe. He is that kind of guy, right?"

"Don't patronize me," Stephanie snapped. "I only came here to discuss this and keep you in line. And you have to promise you won't make a move without me."

"Yeah, yeah, whatever." Glover glanced around, then said on a low voice, "But I guess I should tell you—I've been following him for about a week now."

"Glover!" Stephanie dropped her salad fork, her appetite gone. "I should have known. I had hoped you'd honor my request to leave this alone, but...you don't have any honor, do you?"

"No," he admitted, shaking his head. "And that's the difference between you and me, Stef. I'm willing to get down and dirty to get the best story. While you, you have to be all noble and above reproach.''

''I was taught to be responsible, to live by the Golden Rule.''

''I know—what would Jesus do, right? And where will that get you?'' he said, slurping his drink. ''Where did it get you with Derek Kane?''

''It gets me high ratings and viewer approval,'' she countered, angry that he was turning this into a moral issue. ''And I don't intend to change just to keep up with you, and I won't sink to your level.''

''Then you might be eating my dust,'' Glover replied. ''Now, do you want to know where Derek Kane goes after he works at that oh-so-innocent job of his, or are you going to pull that noble act on me?''

''He goes to work and back home,'' she said, her stomach churning as she willed it to be so.

But Glover wasn't about to let it end there.

''And he goes to visit this same Louise Thomas, twice this week so far. Right after work, both times.''

''So—I told you they're friends. Derek helps out people who need help. He's very...heroic.'' She couldn't tell him just how heroic.

But Glover wasn't buying it anyway. ''Why is he paying her off?''

''He's not paying her off. He's probably just being a good friend. It can't be easy, raising her grand-daughter.''

"And why is she raising that child, anyway?"

"I don't know," Stephanie admitted. "I didn't think it was any of my business to ask. Lots of people raise their grandchildren in today's society."

"Why? Aren't you curious?"

Stephanie sat there remembering the tormented look Derek had given her that day at the church. Did that torment have something to do with Louise and Kendra?

She'd given Derek every opportunity to tell her the truth, to tell her his side of the story. And he'd only held back and then sent her away. What choice did she have, but to stoop to hard-nosed reporter tactics?

And what would it hurt now?

"Want to see if he goes there again today?"

She looked across the table at Glover, hating herself for what she was about to do. "Yes, I think I do. We'll follow him and see if he visits Louise again, but Glover, that doesn't mean he's up to no good."

"It doesn't mean he's the hero you think he is, either," Glover told her as he grabbed his briefcase.

That statement floored Stephanie completely. Had she been so caught up in believing Derek was the perfect hero that she'd become blind to his flaws? Was he keeping secrets because he wanted privacy, or was he deliberately hiding something sinister from the world?

The pain throbbing near her right temple picked up its tempo. Rubbing her forehead, Stephanie willed the pain away, so she could think. She couldn't let Glover get to her. And yet he had.

Stephanie paid the check, then paused to close her eyes. *Lord, I can't believe Derek is corrupt. I won't believe that he's doing something criminal or dishonorable. He cares about people too much. He cares about Louise and Kendra. Help me, Lord, to prove them all wrong. Help me to find the truth, so I can help Derek to heal.*

She'd stand by him, no matter what.

She'd make sure he knew how much she loved him.

And somehow, she'd win him back.

Chapter Thirteen

They were following him again.

Derek hadn't been away from the force so long that he didn't know when he was being tailed. Whoever it was, they were doing a pretty good job. Not too obvious, but definitely there, a few cars away. It was the same car he'd already seen several times this week.

He didn't recognize the car, but the old instincts, the old rage, kicked in as surely as if he were back in Florida, watching his back twenty-four hours a day.

Was the nightmare beginning all over again? Had someone finally figured out just who he really was? Or had Nathan's prediction come true? Was the street gang planning retaliation?

Glad that he'd left the teens with Reverend Byrd

and several members of the congregation back at the church, Derek glanced back into the rearview mirror. "Hey, Laz, we're being tailed. Now, why didn't you alert me?"

The dog whimpered a reply, then laid his head back down on the blanket Derek kept in the small back seat of the pickup's double cab.

"Just kidding, old man. You go on back to sleep. Rest those heavy bones." Derek kept his eyes on the car as it moved closer. "I guess we've both let our guard down lately."

If he hadn't been so distracted by falling for Stephanie Maguire, he might have been more alert himself. After all, he'd never really relaxed since leaving the force.

Then it hit him with the impact of a semitrailer truck.

Stephanie.

She'd said she'd get to the bottom of things. And she certainly hadn't wasted any time. Although the car behind him wasn't hers, he could make out two people inside.

A man and a woman.

A dark-headed woman with hair swirling out around her face. And dark sunshades to cover her eyes.

It didn't help matters to realize that he'd forced her to this. He'd been hurt and stubborn and unyielding, because he just couldn't take the look of sure disgust he'd see in her eyes when he told her the truth. The same disgust he'd seen in Nathan's eyes when the boy had found out that Derek had once been a cop.

He'd wanted to tell her, needed to tell her, so they could get past all of this and just be together.

Derek wanted to be with Stephanie Maguire more than he wanted to take his next breath, but the old fears, the old feelings of self-loathing kept coming in on him, smothering him with shame, choking him with ugly reminders, pushing the growing feelings he had for her out of the way.

She'd said she loved him.

Would she love him after she found out *everything?*

Or would she, too, turn away, the way so many people he'd been close to, people he'd loved, had turned away?

He couldn't risk that. Which is why he'd sent her away before things got worse, before he fell for her completely, before it became too painful to watch her walk away. No, he wasn't ready to risk his heart.

But Stephanie was willing to risk everything, apparently, to find the answers she needed.

Derek stopped his car in front of the modest white wooden house where Louise Thomas lived. Now that he'd broken things off with her, he wouldn't try to stop Stephanie. In fact, maybe *this* was the best way for her to find out the truth.

She'd tracked him here today because she wanted answers. Well, he'd give them to her, face-to-face, to shock her away, the way he'd done the day he'd first kissed her.

And then maybe she'd finally see him for what he really was.

"I think he's spotted us," Stephanie said to Glover, her fingers drumming on the dashboard of Glover's messy economy car. "I told you this was a bad idea."

"And I told you he's up to something," Glover replied, the glee in his words only adding to the sickening feeling in Stephanie's stomach. "Let's just see what he does next."

"He's going to visit his friend," Stephanie snapped, her impatience with Glover's overly dramatic antics getting the best of her.

"Or he's paying someone to keep quiet," Glover said, shifting his gaze from Derek's truck up ahead to her. "Stef, you look pale. Are you all right?"

"I'm getting a headache," she said, willing the nausea to go away.

"Now?" Glover glanced over at her, a brief second of concern coloring his sweaty face. "Did you bring your medicine?"

"I've always got my medicine," she replied, the throbbing near her right eye causing her to see spots.

"I'm okay. Just keep driving. Let's get this over with."

"You haven't had a migraine in a long time. I guess the stress of dealing with Mr. Kane has finally gotten to you, huh?"

"I can deal with the stress, so just drop it."

She wouldn't give in, to either the headache or her worst fears. Derek had every right to visit Louise Thomas. They were friends. They attended church together. And unlike Glover, she refused to believe Derek was doing anything underhanded. She had to believe he was only helping a friend.

And yet she remembered the look he'd given her back at the church. How could she forget the torment, the pain clearly etched on his features each time he looked at little Kendra? What was going on here?

Lord, I believe in him. And I believe You will help me to prove them all wrong. Please, give me the strength to face this, whatever it is, and win Derek's trust and love.

She watched now as Derek pulled the truck up to the curb in front of a small frame house. The home looked clean and neat compared to some of the houses in this neighborhood. Not a safe place to be just when the sun was setting, but Stephanie had been in worse places after dark.

To get the story.

Always to get the story.

She felt sick all over again. This wasn't how she'd wanted to find out about Derek. But then, he hadn't given her much choice, had he?

"We'll just park here," Glover told her, watching as Derek and Lazarus emerged from the truck about half a block in front of them.

"I know he's figured this out," Stephanie said, holding a hand to her head. "Glover, he's not stupid. He was a cop. And I've seen him in action. You don't want to cross him."

"We're not doing anything except sitting here," Glover countered, rolling down a window to get some air into the humid, hot car. "And when he leaves, we can go visit Louise Thomas. Ask her a few questions."

"I will not!"

He looked away from the house Derek had entered, over to Stephanie. "Is this the same Stephanie Maguire who used to spend the entire night out on the street just to get the scoop on a drug bust? Is this the same Stephanie Maguire who camped out in a hotel lobby, just to get an exclusive with that senator who was taking illegal campaign contributions?"

Stephanie had had enough. Maybe because the migraine was winning the battle of hammers in her head, maybe because she felt dirty and awful, sitting here spying on the man she loved. "No, I'm *not* the same," she said now, shouting the words over at

Glover. With a realization that banged inside her head just as heavily as the headache, she clearly saw that that statement was true. "I've changed."

"Oh, boy." Glover kept his eyes on her, giving her a look of utter amazement. "You can't go soft in this business, Stef. You know that."

"I don't care," Stephanie replied. "This is silly. We shouldn't be here. I want to leave. Now, Glover."

"I'm not leaving. I intend to find out what's up with Derek Kane."

"Then I suggest you step out of the car and ask me like a man."

Both Stephanie and Glover looked up in surprise to find Derek standing at Glover's window, glaring down at them. The thundering look of rage on his face only added to the thundering pain inside Stephanie's temple.

Stephanie opened her door and came around the car. "Derek, I'm sorry—"

"No, you're not. This is exactly what you wanted from the beginning, isn't it, Stephanie? Well, you want the truth? I'm going to give it to you."

He took her by the arm, dragging her against him, his eyes the color of heavy smoke. "But only you."

When Glover hopped out of the car, Derek turned to face him, a finger pointed at Glover's nose. "You're not invited. Get back in the car and leave. Now."

"No," Glover said, his voice squeaking in spite of the determined stance he gave. "I won't leave Stephanie with *you*."

"I said get in the car," Derek told him, still holding Stephanie. "Don't make me have to force you back in there."

Stephanie reached out a hand to Glover. "Go, James. I'll be fine. Derek and I need…to clear this up. Alone."

"She's right," Derek said, opening the door for Glover, his action brooking no argument. "We don't need you hovering. Stephanie wanted an exclusive story and I'm going to give her one. You got that, buddy?"

"That's not fair," Glover said, his tone petulant. "I'm the one who brought her here and now she gets the exclusive. I'm on to you, man, and I'm gonna dig until I find out what you've been trying to hide. Landscaping! Yeah, right."

Derek let go of Stephanie then. With one hand he grabbed Glover by the collar of his shirt and forced him inside the car. On a level voice that held more than a threat, he said, "Leave now, while you still have your capped teeth."

Glover gulped, glared up at him, but started the engine. "Stef, do you want me to call the police?"

"She's with a policeman," Derek called. "An ex-one, that is. Which means I don't have to play by the rules anymore.'' He slammed the door shut with a booted foot. ''Now get out of here.''

Stephanie watched as Glover reluctantly drove the car away. ''You certainly know how to win friends and influence people.''

''I'm very good at it.''

Without looking at her, Derek took her by the arm again, guiding her around to the backyard of an abandoned house. He'd obviously used this path to sneak up on them while they'd been arguing.

''Where are we going?'' she asked, more worried about his state of mind than her personal safety. She felt completely safe with Derek, even when he was angry with her. And right now he was extremely angry with her.

''I'm going to show you what you want to see,'' he told her, his features etched in granite, his gaze straight ahead.

They came to a fence. Stephanie could hear a child laughing and talking behind the fence. And a dog playfully barking.

''Derek, please, can't we just talk.'' Her head throbbed so badly, she felt faint, sick to her stomach. And she'd left her purse with her medicine in Glover's car.

This headache had been building for days, and for days she'd ignored it. Sweat popped out on her forehead, and spots danced before her eyes, but she refused to give in to the weakness and nausea. That would be too humiliating. She had to focus on what Derek was trying to tell her. "Derek, let's go somewhere and—"

He turned to her then, placing a hand on each of her shoulders as if he wanted badly to shake her. "I'm done with talking. I'm done with hiding. I want you to see the truth, once and for all. And then, I want you to…just leave me alone."

He pushed her close to the fence, where a broken board gave them access to the backyard. Louise Thomas's backyard.

"It's Kendra," Stephanie whispered, watching through the glare of bright late-afternoon sunshine as the child laughed and splashed water from a small plastic swimming pool while Lazarus barked and stuck his nose in the water. "She's out of her wheelchair."

"Yeah, she's out," Derek said, his voice low and close to Stephanie's ear. "She can sit there and splash in the water. She can even enjoy water therapy at the downtown hospital wellness center. But she can never walk again."

"I'm sorry, Derek, but—"

He placed his arms around Stephanie then, pulling her body back against his as he held her there. With his face close to hers, he whispered in Stephanie's ear. "Take a good long look at that precious little girl, Stephanie, and listen to what I'm about to say to you."

Stephanie swallowed, prayed, felt the tears pricking at her throbbing eyelids, willed the headache to go away. "Derek—"

"I put Kendra in that wheelchair, Stephanie."

Stephanie gasped, then tried to twist around.

"No, don't." He held her tight. "Look at her, not me." His voice became even lower, husky, dangerous and faraway sounding. "I did that. It was my bullet—a bullet from my gun—that paralyzed that child for life."

Because it was so hot, because the headache had now reached monster status, because she thought she was going to surely be sick, Stephanie slumped against Derek. "No, no. I don't believe you."

"It's true," he said, pulling her around to face him at last. "And that's not the half of it. I also killed her father."

The shock, coupled with the utter self-disgust and the old familiar torment she saw so clearly on Derek's face, was too much for Stephanie. The heat took over, the headache won out.

"Oh, no, no," she said on a low moan, understanding pouring over her like liquid fire. Then, because she needed to find a dark, cool spot so she could lie down, she reached up, clinging to Derek's shirt. "I'm going to be—"

Before she could finish, Derek took one look at her face and scooped her up in his arms. Without a word, he carried her around to the front of the house, then entered past the open screen door.

"Louise!"

Stephanie tried to speak, tried to reach a hand up to his face, to the scar on his cheekbone that she loved so much. But Derek only turned his face away from her touch.

She heard footsteps, then a soothing voice. Louise Thomas. With Lazarus, whining a greeting to his master.

"What's wrong, Derek?"

Derek dropped Stephanie on a fluffy couch. "Take care of her, then call her a cab. I've…I've got to get out of here."

Then to Lazarus, "Stay here, boy. Stay with her."

"But Derek—" Louise tried to stop him.

"She knows, Louise. She knows. I told her."

With that, he turned on his heels and left.

The slamming of the screen door echoed through Stephanie's pounding head like a roaring avalanche.

And shattered the last of her resolve.

Chapter Fourteen

She couldn't stop crying. The pain in her head had increased tenfold and the tears had only made it worse, but Stephanie had needed this purging. Needed the soft, matronly voice that had calmed her. Needed the comforting arms that had surrounded her.

Except they hadn't been Derek's arms.

"Now, now, child, it's all right. He'll be back. He loves you so much."

Had she only been dreaming? Or had that been an angel, sent from the Father to reassure her that Derek would forgive her?

She must have dozed off, slept. Now she was awake again, and crying softly. Somewhere near her outstretched hand, a dog whimpered, rubbed his nose to her fingers.

Lazarus. She was safe. Lazarus was here.

The room was blessedly dark, the curtains drawn, the ceiling fan cool against her hot skin.

After Derek had stomped out, Stephanie had tried to go after him. But the nausea had overcome her and she'd only managed to make it to the small bathroom off the hallway.

"Headache," she'd managed to croak out when Louise had handed her a cool rag. "Migraines."

Without a word, the older woman had escorted Stephanie back to the big sofa, bringing pain pills, pillows and a light, lemony-smelling sheet to cover her. "What else can I do for you, honey?"

"Dark. I need it to be dark."

Louise had closed the curtains, turned off the lamps. "I'm going to get Kendra out of the pool. We'll be right back in. You rest now."

But she hadn't been able to rest. And that's when she'd started crying. Then much later someone had comforted her. Someone had prayed for her. And for Derek.

Louise.

Louise was taking care of her, as if Stephanie were the child. And little Kendra was playing quietly now at the small kitchen table, back in her wheelchair.

Wheelchair.

Kendra.

Stephanie groaned as it all came rushing back.

Derek had…had shot Kendra. Had killed her father?

Horrible. Horrible.

Now she understood the torment in his eyes. Now she understood why he watched over Kendra and her grandmother. Now she understood everything. Everything.

Stephanie glanced around. She had to find Derek. Outside, night had come. A humid summer night with fireflies and crickets, with a hot wind blowing and the sounds of the city off in the distance.

Down on the floor, by her hand, Lazarus lay looking up at her with his doleful eyes. She reached for him. He whimpered and licked her hand again. Stephanie automatically patted the big dog's head, grateful to find him here. Maybe that meant Derek was nearby, too, since he never let the dog out of his sight.

But maybe he'd done that this time. Maybe he wouldn't be back, ever.

Yet he'd left Lazarus to watch over her. That gave her hope and brought fresh tears to her eyes.

"How long have I been here?" she asked Louise, her voice sounding like dry twigs against a tin roof as it scratched across the raw nerve endings of her mind.

Louise turned from the stove, where a single light burned. Coming around the small kitchen counter, she reached for Stephanie's hand. "About two hours. Do you feel any better, sugar?"

"It hurts," Stephanie said, although she didn't just mean the headache. Her whole being hurt. This hurt cut deep into her soul.

"It was an accident," Louise said at last. "A terrible accident. But he can't forgive himself."

Stephanie let that soak in, while a fresh batch of tears soaked the front of her cotton blouse. She'd never cried this much—not since her father had died. She'd never cried over anything or anyone this much.

But this—this wasn't fair. This wasn't the way life was supposed to be. Derek was a good man. A good man. Oh, how he must have suffered with this.

She clung to Louise's hand. "Can you tell me what happened?"

Louise sank into the chair beside the couch, squeezing Stephanie's hand. In the next second, Lazarus alerted, his head going up, his nose sniffing the air as he let out a little half bark.

Then they heard footsteps hitting the porch. The screen door opened and a shadow sliced through the single light shining from the kitchen stove. Derek stood in the hallway, his features etched in darkness, his eyes locking with Stephanie's in that one ray of light.

Stephanie's heart hammered a beat that matched the racking pain in her head. He'd come back! God had heard her pleas and brought Derek back to her. She couldn't move, couldn't take her eyes away from his.

Louise gave Stephanie a look filled with both pain and triumph. "I think Derek should be the one to explain all of this to you. It's Kendra's bedtime, anyway."

With that, she took Kendra, who had remained quiet and watchful while the adults talked, and started up the small hallway toward the bedrooms.

But Kendra halted her grandmother when they reached the spot where Derek was standing. Reaching up, the child took Derek's hand in hers. In a small voice that cut through the still night like a lace curtain fluttering at an open window, she said, "I love you, Mr. Derek."

Derek brushed a hand across his eyes, then squatted down in front of Kendra's chair. In a raw, low voice, he said, "I love you, too, baby."

Then he let go of Kendra's hand and stood, wrapping his arms across his chest as if to stifle the pain.

Stephanie sat up, held out her own hand. "Derek?"

He looked over at her, then closed the distance between them. Sinking down beside her, he took her into his arms and held her tightly to him. "I'm sorry, Stephanie."

"Derek, don't be, please don't be."

She held him to her, her tears drenching his shirt, his tears moistening her hair.

"I'm sorry I came back. I meant to stay away. But…I couldn't."

"Don't say that. I don't want you to stay away. I want to help you."

"How can anyone help me?" he asked, lifting his head to stare into her eyes. "How can you say that when seeing what I did made you physically ill?"

Stephanie touched a hand to his face, willing the tension, the hurt, to go away. "Derek, no. I have a migraine. It had already started when we followed you here and it…it got worse from the heat and—"

"And from hearing my confession," he finished, pushing her hand away. "I make you sick."

"No, no." She sat up, ignoring the throbbing pulse that threatened to split her head in two. "I was already sick from the headache. Derek, is that what you thought? That I was so repulsed, I got sick?"

"I saw your face, Stephanie. You were in shock."

"Of course I was shocked," she admitted, finding her strength through sheer will. "But Derek, I know you didn't mean any of this to happen. I believe it was an accident, like Louise said."

He sank back on the couch, then ran a hand over his face. "Yeah, a horrible accident. In a split second, my life changed, Kendra's life changed and my whole world became one nightmare of pain and regret."

"And you're still living in that nightmare."

He let out a breath, put his hands down on his knees. "I thought I was doing pretty good. I thought I'd found some peace at last."

"And then I came along."

He shot her a wry smile. "And then you came along."

"I'm sorry."

"You don't need to apologize. I should have told you the truth that first night, but I thought I could handle this."

"Why don't you tell me the whole story now?"

Derek looked over at Stephanie. It wasn't hard to see the pain etched in her eyes, even there in the darkness of the still, quiet room. Whether the dark circles were from the headache or the pain he'd caused her, he couldn't be sure. Could he hurt her any more by telling her the whole ugly story? Could he trust her to keep it off the record?

He knew the answers to both those questions.

He had to trust her. He loved her. But he wouldn't risk hurting her ever again. And he wouldn't risk losing her. He'd tell his story, and then he'd leave her alone, now, while they both still had time to recover. Now, before they were both in too deep.

Ignoring that little voice that told him he was already too deeply involved with Stephanie Maguire to turn back, he cleared his throat and started talking, his voice calm and level, his gaze drifting out into the night.

"I joined the police force in a small town near Tallahassee, Florida, when I was around twenty-three or twenty-four. I was so proud to be a police officer, so glad that I'd escaped having to be a farmer like my father and my brothers. I thought I'd make something of myself, work my way up to being a big-city cop."

"How long were you a cop?"

"About four years." He stretched his long legs, locked his hands behind his head, remembering. "I was good at my job. Soon I was working the narcotics division, coordinating drug stings with some of the bigger cities. You know, trying to stop drug trafficking on the interstates. We got this tip about a major drug deal going down in our jurisdiction, so we went out that night intent on making some arrests."

He stopped, breathed deeply, put his hands down on his knees again. "But things went bad. We were in the backwoods off the interstate—more like a swamp. Bugs and other critters everywhere, and marshland so dense you could get lost in it forever. It wasn't the best place to be, but that's where things were happening, so we went in."

He described how they'd walked through the dense swamp to the spot the informant had indicated, how they'd silently set up the whole nocturnal operation, and waited for the suspects to arrive and make their move.

And then the team had announced themselves and told the two suspects they were under arrest.

"One of the suspects started firing on us and we returned fire. It was all over in about two minutes."

Derek had to stop, to catch his breath again. The nightmares were so real. "The suspect fired directly at me, and I returned fire. He was crouching by his vehicle and at first I couldn't get a clear shot. He kept firing, in spite of our shouts for him to drop his weapon. A bullet whizzed by my face—that's how I got this scar." He briefly touched the white dent on his cheekbone. "I returned fire once more, and the suspect went down. Then everything went still. I'll never forget the quietness after all that gunfire."

Derek heard Stephanie's sharp gasp. Would she be sick again? He felt sick himself. He wiped his clammy palms against the denim of his jeans, then placed his head in his hands. "It was all over. We arrested one suspect, then went to check on the other one. He was already dead." Swallowing hard, he forced himself to continue. "That's when we heard...someone crying inside the car."

Stephanie brought a hand to her mouth. "Oh, Derek."

Derek looked across at her, hoping to calm her, but before he could move, Stephanie was pulling his hands away from his face, taking him back in her arms. "Oh, Derek. You didn't know. How could you know?"

He pushed her away, self-disgust putting an effective shield between him and the pain and pity he saw in her eyes. "You're right. I didn't know. None of us knew. The man had his child in the car with him. A little five-year-old girl. His daughter."

"Kendra."

Stephanie was crying again now. Those tears pierced at Derek's consciousness like nails hitting skin. The old humiliation, the old remorse and guilt that had never really gone away, came back full force.

"Kendra," he said, his voice a whisper. "A little girl, out for a ride with her father. He was going to make the drop, then take her for ice cream. She kept telling us that when they were putting her in the ambulance. She kept saying, 'My daddy's gonna take me for ice cream. Where's my daddy?'"

He let out a shuddering breath. "How do you tell a kid so young, so innocent, that her daddy is dead, that you killed him and accidentally shot her?"

Derek watched as Stephanie tried to stand. She probably didn't want to be in the same room with him.

He pushed her back down, his hands gripping the couch above her shoulders, his face inches from hers. "Now do you understand? Do you?" When she nodded, he continued. "I killed Kendra's father. And I shot her, too. Her mother died from an overdose long ago. She had no one. No one. And she was lying in that hospital room calling out for her daddy." He sank back down. "Because of me, that child was all alone in the world."

"Except for her grandmother," Stephanie said.

"Yes. Her grandmother here in Atlanta. So I watched over her, tried to visit her at the hospital, got in touch with Louise.

"Then they took me off the force, suspended me indefinitely while internal affairs conducted its investigation. And the press took the story and ran with it. I was branded a racist, a killer, and every other vile name you can think of. But none of those names could describe the self-loathing I felt inside. And it didn't matter how many times I talked to the department shrink. I hated myself, hated what I'd done. Then, to make matters worse, I was considered unstable, not fit to do my job.

"I got death threats, and believe me, I prayed they'd make good on their threats. I wanted to die. I prayed over and over for God to take me and give Kendra her life back, give her the ability to walk again."

Stephanie tried to reach for him, but this time he got up, putting some distance between them. Because Derek knew, if he let her hold him again, he'd never let go. He just wanted to get through this, tell her the truth finally, and then leave.

"Then Louise came to see me. She told me she didn't blame me for her son's death or Kendra's condition, told me she had forgiven me. And she told me she was bringing Kendra here to Atlanta, to live with her."

"And you followed them here?"

He nodded. "I was cleared of any wrongdoing, but the damage had been done. The press, the hate-mongers, the criminals, they all hounded me. And the rest of the force worried that I'd lose it completely. They claimed I'd lost my instincts, that I'd never be able to fire a gun again." He shrugged. "Who knows, maybe they were right. I haven't picked up a gun since that night. I resigned from the police force and came to Atlanta. I had to see Kendra, make sure she was all right."

He paced around the small room, then looked down at Stephanie, his hands shoved in the pockets of his jeans. "On my first visit, Louise told me about her son's long history with drugs. Told me how she'd prayed for him, tried to help him. But it was too late for that now.

"Then she told me about Miss Nadine. Said she was looking for a new gardener." He let out a little snort. "I told her I didn't know much about formal gardens, just vegetable gardening and farming, but she was determined that I go and talk to Miss

Nadine. Then Louise invited me to church with her—her old country church, far from the city.''

"So you rebuilt your life."

"I tried. I started working for Miss Nadine, with only a strong back and an even stronger determination. I read books about landscaping and watched all those shows on cable—how-to shows, took classes on horticulture and landscaping at the local college." He shrugged again, shoved his hands even deeper into his pockets. "But…I found a certain peace being alone out in the sunshine, working with my hands. I felt safe with the plants and trees, the sunshine and rain. And I loved the hard work, and I liked being able to talk to God, pray to Him while I went about my work. It helped me to sleep at night.

"Then Miss Nadine recommended me to a couple of her friends. I took a master gardener's class and took some more business classes. After about a year or so, I opened my own landscaping business, working with wholesale nurseries, working from a trailer on the lake."

"Just you and Lazarus."

At the mention of his name, Lazarus whimpered and went back to sleep. Derek watched as Stephanie rubbed the dog's head, his heart burning with a heated pain at the simple beauty of the woman he loved petting his dog.

"I found Lazarus out on the road. Someone had dropped him off, half dead and flea-bitten. I poured my heart into keeping him alive, and training him. For some reason, I believed God had sent Lazarus to me, to make me feel safe again.'' He stopped, threw up a hand. ''I had worked with some of the K-9 officers back in Florida. One of them transferred up here and he helped me train Laz. He's my friend on the force here.''

''So you had your life back on track.''

''Yes, I guess I did. Soon business was good, and I felt forgiven, almost. I got involved with the intervention program, working with troubled youths. That helped ease some of my guilt, I guess. I started building my house, and helped to pay for Kendra's therapy and medicine. And I'm going to put that little girl through college, too. That's why I was downtown the night we met. I was getting all of this straight with my lawyer.''

''I believe you.''

He turned to her then, fell on his knees in front of her. ''But do you believe that I'll ever be forgiven? I mean really forgiven? Do you believe that you can love a man like me? Can you get past all of this—what I did? Can you?''

''I believe God has already forgiven you, Derek,'' she told him, trying to reach out to him. ''And I believe I can love you. I already do.''

He rose, whirled on his booted feet. ''I didn't come back here for this, Stephanie. I only came back to explain things, to make you see why I didn't want to be put on the spot, why I couldn't be hailed a hero.''

"You don't think you deserve hero status."

"No, I don't think I deserve any kind of status."

"So you'll keep on punishing yourself for something that was beyond your control? You'll push me away, simply because you don't think you deserve any happiness?''

"I'm pushing you away because it can never work between us. And I knew that from the beginning."

"You really believe that, without even giving us a chance?''

He turned to stare down at her. She looked so fragile, so very beautiful, sitting there on the couch. Her eyes were swollen from tears and pain, her hair was limp and tousled, and her heart was breaking. He could see that clearly enough. And that's what stayed with him, worried him. He couldn't take the pain he saw there in her eyes.

"*This* would always be there, between us. I couldn't take it. The looks of disgust, the wondering. I won't have you thinking that you're in love with a killer."

"I'm in love with a good, noble man," she said. "Derek, you acted in self-defense. You were trained to fire with deadly intent." She lifted her head, her eyes finding his. "And I think I love you even more now than I did before."

But Derek couldn't accept that. He didn't want sympathy or pity, both of which he was sure she was feeling toward him right now.

"No," he replied, signaling for Lazarus. "I'm going to take you home, Stephanie. And then I want you to forget about me. Forget this whole ugly story. It's the best thing for both of us, and it's the way it has to be."

She got up then, facing him nose-to-nose. "Why, Derek? To spare *my* feelings? Or to protect *yourself* from being hurt again?"

Chapter Fifteen

He didn't answer her question. He simply ushered her out the door, calling good-night to Louise as he went. Then he drove her to her apartment, silent all the way.

At the door, still reeling from her headache and everything Derek had told her, Stephanie tried to reason with him. "Derek, come inside and we can talk."

Looking down at the floor, he shook his head. "No. You need to take your medicine and get some rest."

"So you'll just leave me here, with this headache, with nothing settled between us."

He touched a hand to her temple, the tenderness in the gesture warming her heart. "I'm sorry about your headache, Stephanie, but as for the rest, it's settled already. It was settled the night we met.''

"I should have just left things alone. That's what you're saying. I should have left you alone, in spite of my feelings for you?"

"Yes."

Stephanie realized this was all she'd get out of him tonight. Derek was still too caught up in his past to see that he might have a future with her, if he could forgive himself.

Well, she'd back down for now, but this was far from over. She'd prove it to him somehow. For now, she just needed to get rid of this pain in her head, and the horrible images centered there right along with it.

She turned to open her door, then realized her keys were in her purse, which she'd left in Glover's car.

"Oh, no," she said, whirling to stare up at Derek.

"What?" He grabbed her, concern coloring his face.

"Glover has my purse."

"Can't you get the apartment manager or a maintenance man? Or do you want me to break the door down?"

"Yes, no!" She frantically pushed her hair off her face.

"I'm not worried about getting in right now. Derek, I carry computer disks in my purse. Current files on the stories I'm working on. I bring them home to work on my computer here…and I have a disk—a file on *you*.''

He frowned, realization clouding his eyes. ''So. Glover doesn't know anything and neither did you until tonight.'' Then his expression changed. ''Did you?''

His words sliced through the pain of her headache, causing an even worse ache. He still didn't trust her.

''No, but…Glover doesn't know you were the Good Samaritan. I never told him. If he puts everything together—''

''And it's on the disk, right?''

At her nod, he groaned. ''Oh, boy.''

''Maybe he won't find anything.''

''And maybe he's just the type to search until he does.''

Stephanie tried to push past him. ''I have to go and find him, get my purse back.''

''Whoa, wait a minute.'' Derek pulled her close, then stood her against the wall, a hand on either side of her face. ''You're in no condition to go anywhere. You're about to fall over as it is.''

''I have to stop him.'' Stephanie pushed at Derek's chest with her hands, but he only drew her closer.

Too close. And they both knew it.

He stared down at her, his gaze moving across

her face with a desperate caress. "I don't care about that right now."

Stephanie looked up into his eyes and saw the truth hidden there in the gray depths. He loved her. He just didn't want to admit that love. He was fighting against it with his look, his touch, his whole being. Derek held her there, so close she could feel his breath on her throat, so close she could have touched her lips to the white scar centered against his dark skin. Just a kiss away, yet so far, so far out of her reach.

She wouldn't lose him.

But right now she had to hurry him away so she could save him from Glover's ambitious ideas. If the real story broke, they'd both lose. She'd fail and she'd lose Derek forever.

So she tried to break away from the unbearable tenderness of his touch.

"I'll go get the manager to let me in," she said, breathless. And then she'd sneak back out when Derek was gone.

"Not just yet."

"But—"

"I just want one last kiss," he told her. "I know it's wrong. I shouldn't ask for it. I shouldn't feel this way, but I can't help myself. Just one last kiss, Stephanie."

"No," she said, pain slicing through her head and heart. "I won't let you shock me ever again, Derek.

And I won't let you kiss me, and then just walk away. Not this time.''

"But you were the one who ran away the first time, remember?"

"Yes, and that's precisely my point. You were finally honest with me tonight. You had to relive all the horror, all the pain of what happened all those years ago." She stopped, her gaze locking with his. "You tell me all of this, then expect me to be able to just let you go. It's over, finished, just like that? But now you want to kiss me goodbye, when I want to kiss you hello. We could start fresh, Derek. If you'd only trust me."

The blankness covering his face looked like a character sketch on a suspect—everything was there, but nothing was readable. "It has to be this way, Stephanie."

"No, it doesn't. The next time you kiss me, I want it to be because you want to be with me, not because you're trying to scare me away, not because you're telling me goodbye. But because you want me, Derek."

He dropped his head forward, closed his eyes, swallowed. "You'll never know all the things I want, Stephanie."

"I think I have a good idea," she told him. "I just wish one of those things could be me."

Letting out a frustrated sigh, Derek said, "Right now I need to kiss you. And you're refusing me?"

She heard the desperation in that request, felt that same desperation in her soul. But he would break her completely if he kissed her. She'd beg him not to go.

And she would not beg.

"Yes. I'm refusing because you told me it's over between us. But it isn't. It can never be over, because I love you."

He backed away then, his face going from tender to tortured. "You don't love me. You love this image of the perfect hero. Based on your father, based on your own romantic notions—I don't know. But it isn't love for me, Stephanie. And if I stayed, you'd see that soon enough."

"Do you think I'm that shallow, that superficial?"

"I think you're in love with love, with some such notion of a perfect hero, and that's not me."

"Then go," she said, shoving him away. "Just go, Derek. Go be miserable and lonely." Pushing past him, she called over her shoulder, "I'm going to find the apartment manager to let me in. You don't have to wait."

"I won't leave you—you're sick."

With that, he grabbed her by the arm and headed back down the hallway toward the elevators, pulling her with him. "We'll find the manager together or I'll bust the door down, then you're going inside that apartment and you're going to bed."

She didn't argue with him. She knew him well enough by now to understand it wouldn't work. Not tonight.

When this is all over, Stephanie thought, clutching the nearest wall for support, I'm going to prove you wrong, Derek. I'm going to prove that I love you and only you.

But first she had to find Glover and stop him.

After tracking down the maintenance man to let her in, Stephanie pushed out of her mind the image of Derek walking down the lonely hallway toward the elevators, then rushed to the phone, only to find a message blinking there. It was Glover.

"Hey, are you all right? Did that madman hurt you? Call me. I'm at the station."

He was at the station, at midnight. She had to go and find him. Glover would be digging, searching, calling in all his sources. And if he'd read her file on Derek, he'd know why she'd tried so hard to protect Derek, too.

Willing the pain in her head to go away, Stephanie tried the nose spray the doctor had prescribed for migraines. Then she took a hot shower, donned some jeans and a T-shirt and called a cab, since her car was still at the television station.

The cab ride provided a chance for her to shut her eyes for a few minutes, while the medicine kicked in. The pain dulled to a distant throb, but refused to give up.

And so did she.

It was around one in the morning when she found Glover hard at work at his little cubicle. All around them, the place continued to buzz and hum, regardless of the late hour. The news division never shut down. Before, Stephanie would have buzzed and hummed right along with it. But now, now she was so very tired.

"Stephanie!" James came up out of his chair, whether from relief or despair, Stephanie couldn't be sure. "Are you okay? You look kinda pale."

"Headache," she said, straining to see what he was working on. "What's up?"

"What are you doing here if you feel so bad? Did that crazy ex-cop upset you?"

He hadn't even bothered asking her what she'd found out. Maybe because he already knew.

"You left me a message. What are *you* doing, Glover?"

He rolled his eyes, then pressed his meaty hands to his shoulder, rubbing hard. "Do you have to ask?"

Stephanie sank into the nearest chair, her fingers automatically going to her temples in her own massage. "You're determined to get the goods on Derek Kane, right?"

Glover nodded. "And you were determined to

keep everything from me. I know who he is, Stephanie.''

Not wanting to give anything away, Stephanie watched his face. He might be bluffing. "Oh, and who is he?"

"Your Good Samaritan," Glover said, a smug smile creeping across his face.

"You read my files, you snake!"

"No, oh, no." He held up a hand. "When I got back to work and told Claire who you were with, and how Kane had practically forced me to get lost, she panicked and told me about the night you two met. Told me you had a thing for Mr. Kane, a bad crush that was clouding your judgment and interfering with your work."

"That is not true!" A pale rage rolled like a thunderstorm throughout Stephanie's tense system. "Claire had no right to tell you anything about Derek. It's personal."

"She thought she was doing you a favor," Glover explained. "She's worried about you. Thinks you lost your objectivity with this one."

"No, she's worried about ratings," Stephanie replied, the sick feeling in her stomach doubling. If Claire was willing to tell Glover that, she'd be willing to run the whole story, regardless of how Stephanie felt.

And Stephanie could just hear the tease.

"Local Good Samaritan was once branded a trigger-happy cop, killing a father and crippling an innocent child for life. Details at eleven.''

Stephanie knew because once, she would have written the lead exactly that way herself. To get ratings, to draw in more viewers with titillating details. But not anymore.

Not anymore, Lord, she pledged. God had brought Derek and her together, and now she understood why. Derek needed her, to help him heal. And she needed Derek, to help her find her own humanity.

Oh, Father, thank you. Help me, help me to find a way to save both of us. I love him, Lord. I truly love him.

''Glover, I'm asking you as a friend to stop with this story. There's nothing to tell.''

''I think you're wrong there, Stef.'' He held up a printout. ''Your so-called Good Samaritan has a rather interesting past.''

Stephanie felt the room shifting. ''What do you mean?''

''I mean, Mr. Kane isn't the only one with friends in high places. I've got an in at the police department myself.''

''So. I have connections there, too, but I didn't find anything on Derek.''

''Maybe you've got the wrong connections.''

''What are you trying to tell me, Glover?''

''That your macho man was indeed once a cop

down in sunny Florida, but he lost his job because of a nasty incident involving a drug bust.''

Stephanie tried to remain calm as she willed a blankness over her face. ''Yes, he was a cop, but he's retired now.''

''And do you know why he got fired?''

''He wasn't fired. He resigned.''

''Under a cloud of suspicion, according to my source.''

''Well, your source is wrong.''

''Why are you so intent on defending this man?''

''Why are you so intent on destroying him? This is a nonstory, Glover. It was over long before it started.''

''Don't you think people have a right to know that a man you held up as an example of a Good Samaritan has a past that is checkered with shady doings?''

Stephanie watched his face and saw the greed plastered right there with the beads of sweat and day-old beard growth. How could she have ever trusted Glover at all?

Deciding he was fishing for either more information or a confirmation of what he already had, she shrugged. ''I think Derek Kane is a good man. And I think you're barking up the wrong tree.''

''Sure, and that's why you came back downtown in the middle of the night. Just to tell me that.''

''Yes.''

"Well, if *you* won't give me the facts, I'll find out everything I need to know first thing in the morning. I called our affiliate in Tallahassee. They did some digging. They have the whole story on tape."

Stephanie got up to lean down at him. "You can't do that."

"I'm going to do it, and you have no right to stop me. It'll air on tomorrow night's broadcast." He stood up then. "So I suggest you go home and sleep off that headache. Things will be hopping around here in the morning."

Stephanie saw her purse lying in her own cubicle. "Why didn't you just take my files, since you obviously don't have a lick of scruples anyway?"

"I checked them," he admitted as he grabbed his coat. "But by then Claire had verified everything on them anyway. And you didn't seem to have the complete story. I do believe you're getting soft, Stephanie."

"Why are you doing this?" she asked again.

"You really don't get it, do you?" His expression went from greedy to bitter, sending a little chill of warning down Stephanie's spine. "It's always been about you, Stephanie. Stephanie Maguire, the star of WNT. You could do no wrong, and no matter how I tried to catch up with you, you still managed to get all the glory."

His disgust with her was apparent in the way he

snapped his next words. "And to top things off, you wouldn't even give me the time of day. Had to keep things professional between *us*. Then along comes your idea of the perfect hero—Mr. Derek Kane. Well, I'm going to show both of you that sometimes the so-called good guys don't always win."

Shocked and repulsed, Stephanie could only shake her head. "So you're doing this out of some sense of revenge? You're jealous of me, and angry because I didn't accept your advances, because I didn't fall head over heels for you?"

"Something like that."

"I'll fight you on this, Glover," she retorted as she grabbed her duffel bag purse. "I won't let you run this story. It's wrong. And you're doing it for all the wrong reasons."

"Too late, Stef. Claire has already approved it."

Late the next day, Derek heard a car pulling up the driveway to his house. Lazarus barked a greeting as Stephanie stepped out of her little sports car and hurried up onto the deck, a black videotape clutched in her hand. She looked tired, completely drained.

Maybe it was from the headache, but from the look in her eyes, Derek got a gut reaction it was something more.

He met her out on the deck. "Hey. What are you doing here?"

Without preamble, she said, "I have to tell you

something—about what happened today, about what's going to happen tonight.'' Then she shoved the tape into his hand. "And I want you to look at this…later.''

Derek felt his whole world going red with a rage of despair. "So, talk,'' he said, already figuring what she was going to say.

Before she could get out the next words, a van pulled up in the driveway beside Stephanie's car— a WNT news van with her co-worker James Glover inside. And behind that, a car from another station. Then a car with the *Atlanta Journal and Constitution* logo plastered on its side.

Reporters. After him again. They'd found out.

Spotting the approaching cameras, Stephanie gave him a pleading look. "The story broke on the six-o'clock news—just a teaser, but it was enough to bring out—''

Glover rushed up, interrupting her. "Mr. Kane, care to tell us about your days as a police officer down in Florida? Can you explain why your heroic deeds of a few weeks ago don't quite add up with what happened when you left the force?''

"He doesn't want to comment,'' Stephanie said, pushing at Glover. "Get out of here.''

She turned back to Derek. "Please—''

"You don't need to explain,'' he said, already backing into the house while Glover shouted at him to give a statement. Giving Stephanie a reluctant look, he added, "You did what you had to do, I guess. You didn't break the story, but that sure didn't stop you from giving your friend here the go-ahead. Now leave."

"Derek? No, please listen to me—"

But he didn't want to listen. Derek slammed the door, threw down the tape she'd handed him, then immediately began pulling the blinds shut, blocking out the view, blocking out the peace he'd known these past few years, blocking out Stephanie's look of regret and longing.

And love.

Two days later Stephanie stood on the long back porch of her mother's cabin in the Blue Ridge mountains. All around her the vista of blue-green spruce trees and mountain laurel cast out a picture of breathtaking beauty, the waning sun coloring the woods and valleys in tranquil shades of silver, blue and gold.

But Stephanie could find no tranquillity in these timeless mountains. And no matter how hard she prayed, she could find no peace.

Not without Derek. Not without his love and his trust.

"I failed him, Lord," she whispered to the wind that played with her mother's tinkling pewter butterfly chimes. "I let Derek down and now I've lost him forever."

"Oh, I don't know about that."

She turned to find him standing there on one corner of the wraparound porch. Standing in the shadows, his face hidden from the light.

Stephanie held her hands to her stomach, tears forming in her eyes. Tears that she refused to cry. "How did you find me?"

"I used to be a cop, remember? I tracked down that hotshot news producer with the dangly earrings. She told me you might be here. And luckily, your mother's number is listed in the local phone book."

"You spoke to Claire?"

The shadow of his head moved as he lifted his chin. "Yeah. We got a few things straight between us."

"And you called my mother?"

"Uh-huh. She's gone for a long walk now, with my sappy dog. He always falls for pretty ladies."

Stephanie refused to hope. But her heart danced toward him anyway. "What are you doing here, Derek?"

"I'm not sure, really. Except to say my place has been a little crowded over the last few days."

"I'm so sorry—"

He held up a hand. "It took me a while, but I finally got it, what with Miss Nadine's blunt observations and Louise's gentle prayers and none-too-gentle persuasion. And mainly because of the truth my heart kept telling me. You didn't help put out the story on me. You wouldn't do that to the man you love.''

Stephanie clutched her hands to her stomach, fighting the need to rush headlong into his arms. ''No, I wouldn't. I fought them, Derek.''

''And did your own version of the story.''

She let out a breath, clutched her stomach even more tightly. ''Did you look at the tape I gave you?''

''Uh-huh.''

''I begged Claire to run my version, but she said it was too soft, too one-sided. So I brought the tape to you instead.''

''After you resigned,'' he said, his nod moving in the shadows. ''Oh, yeah, that's on the news right along with my story—or I should say your story. You see, I convinced Ms. Cook to run the tape you gave me.'' He stood there, silent and still. ''You certainly made me out to be that hero you wanted— almost convinced even *me* I'm an okay person. Half of Atlanta is cheering for me and the other half doesn't know what to make of either one of us. We certainly make a pair, don't we?''

Stephanie's heart rose and opened like a flower in the morning dew. He'd forced Claire to run that tape, not to redeem himself, but to show Stephanie that he understood. That he cared, after all. He'd done it for her sake.

He was still in the shadows. She wanted him to come out into the light, with her, forever.

"I do love you, Derek," she said, the tears falling freely now. "I begged them not to do this. When they refused, I had to resign. I couldn't let them destroy you all over again."

"You are a very noble person."

"No, no, I'm not. I just couldn't deal with it anymore. And I'm sorry I brought this on you."

"So you gave up the work you love, to save me from the scrutiny of the press." He shrugged, shifted a foot. "Little good that did you. Now you're out of a job."

"I'll find other work. But I might not ever find another man like you."

He lifted his hand again. "I'm not a hero. As long as you understand that—"

"I do." She moved a step closer. "But you need to understand something, too. You will always, always be my hero, regardless of what the press or anyone else says. You came to my rescue, in more ways than I can ever explain. And I'll fight for you, Derek."

His next words were wry and bittersweet. "Then I have to tell you something."

"What?"

"You're the one who did the rescuing. You rescued me from myself. Now that everything's out in the open, I don't have to hide anymore. I'll always regret what happened, but now I can move on. And I can finally accept forgiveness. I didn't want to see that at first, but now I do."

Stephanie gulped back tears. "We'll get through this together, with God's love and grace, if you'll let me help you."

"Please don't cry," he said, his voice as soothing as a gentle rain. "It's okay. Believe it or not, I've had some pretty strong allies this week. Miss Nadine gave a statement to the press, a testament, really. Called me a good man and said everyone needed to pray hard and mind their own business. And recommended me as a fine gardener, too."

"That should carry some weight."

"It did. *With me.*" He looked away, then back at her. "And Louise, Kendra, Reverend Byrd, even my two lovable wards—they all vouched for me."

"You have a flock of angels watching over you."

"Maybe. But I never knew just how much I depended on my church family, until now."

She didn't dare move toward him, for fear that he'd disappear. Or push her away. So she just stood there, her voice quivering as she tried to explain everything in her heart.

"I...I want you to know you can depend on me, too, Derek. You're...you're like this beautiful forest animal, caught in a trap. When I try to reach out and help you, you snarl and fight at me, because you're afraid. I just want so badly to love you, to touch that scar on your face, and the scar in your heart.''

He stepped around the corner then, his eyes wet with tears, his hand reaching out to her across the planked porch. ''Come here.''

With that, she ran to him, wrapping her arms around him. They held each other for a long time, then he took one of her hands in his and held it to his face.

''Touch me, Stephanie. Right here.'' He placed her hand on the jagged scar, then closed his eyes. When he opened them, she saw a gentle peace shining through the deep gray.

Stephanie pressed her fingers there, tracing the shattered pattern of the scar, then she moved her hand and touched her lips to the brand he carried on the surface. With her other hand she touched his chest, finding his heartbeat. ''And here,'' she said. ''Can I ever touch you here, in your heart, Derek?''

''I think you did that the first time I saw you,'' he said, his lips moving toward hers. ''I love you, Stephanie.''

He kissed her hello.

The butterfly wind chimes moved in a timeless melody that spoke of a new beginning, a rebirth. Off in the distance they heard Lazarus's bark mixing with the sound of her mother's laughter.

Derek smiled at Stephanie as they watched the sun sink toward the mountains, then slowly settle behind the golden peaks. With the gloaming came the peace for which they had both been searching.

The promise of God's love surrounded them, steadfast and sure, as they held each other and found a light in the darkness.

Epilogue

"And now it brings me great pleasure and immense honor to present Derek Kane with the Atlanta Humanitarian of the Year Award."

The mayor of Atlanta stepped back from the podium as Derek came forward in the brilliant fall sunlight. Applause erupted from the large group gathered in Nadine Hamilton's backyard, while news cameras flashed and microphones echoed the clapping.

Derek glanced around, gave a sheepish grin, then spoke out into the crowd. "Thank you, Mr. Mayor. And thanks to Miss Nadine Hamilton and the women of the garden club for nominating me for this award. I don't believe I deserve this, but my wife, Stephanie, says that I should accept it anyway."

While everyone laughed and clapped, he stopped, looked around at the woman sitting beside the mayor. The woman he loved.

"It started out tough for us. But we made it through with God's redeeming love, with the support of our friends and family, and with the knowledge that what we decided to do with our combined experience would benefit Atlanta. Through Kendra's Children, our intervention program for troubled teens, we've managed to help many of the youths of Atlanta stay away from drugs and crime and become more productive citizens."

As the crowd applauded again, he lifted a hand to two other people sitting on the podium next to Stephanie. "And today, we have two examples of the program with us. Marco Stanley and Nathan Hayes will both be attending college this fall."

The applause broke out all over again, and Derek nodded and smiled. "It hasn't been easy for these two, but through our mentoring program, they learned self-respect, self-discipline, and they learned that we love them and want to help them. They turned away from crime and turned toward God. And for that, we salute them."

Out in the crowd, Louise and Kendra smiled and clapped right along with Miss Nadine and the entire congregation from the Church of Flowery Branch, while Lazarus barked his own approval.

As the crowd cheered, Derek went across the

stage and gave each youth a hug. Marco hugged him back in a tight grip, while Nathan gave him a loose embrace.

But Derek saw the gleam of admiration and pride in Nathan's eyes. It was more than he'd ever dreamed possible.

The past year and a half had been more than he'd ever hoped for. He'd married the woman he loved, and together, they had put the gang festering in Marco and Nathan's neighborhood out of commission. Stephanie had written and produced an award-winning documentary on the subject and now had offers coming in from all over the country asking for her journalistic skills.

But that would have to wait a while.

Derek came back to the podium. "I'd like to recognize my wife, Stephanie Maguire Kane." He motioned for her to stand up. "Come here," he said, smiling at the girth of her pregnancy as she pushed herself off her chair and slowly moved across the stage. She looked so beautiful, he had to catch his breath.

Then he turned back to the laughing crowd. "As you can see, we've been busy and blessed. Any day now, we're expecting our first child."

Stephanie hugged him, then said something into his ear.

On a rush of breath, Derek shouted into the mike. "Make that *right now*. My wife just told me she thinks she's in labor. Uh...thank you again for this award, but we have to get to the hospital."

With that, everyone went into action. "Do you need a police escort?" the mayor asked as Derek helped Stephanie off the stage.

Before Derek could answer, Stephanie smiled over at her husband. "No, thanks. I've got one."

As the crowd parted with everyone shouting good wishes, Derek turned to his wife. "I'm an *ex*-cop, remember?"

Stephanie groaned, grimacing with another contraction. Then she touched a hand to the scar on his face, her smile radiant and confident. "Yeah, I remember. But I think you can use all that training and instinct to get me to the hospital before Miss Nadine tries to birth this baby right here in the same spot where we got married."

"You want me to speed? Break the law?" He'd run every red light in the city if he had to, and they both knew it.

She gripped his chin, determination shining in her eyes while pain colored her complexion. "I want you to do whatever it takes, and soon. Your son is about to be born."

He grinned. "Yes, ma'am."

Stephanie kissed him on the mouth. "That's my hero."

* * * * *

Dear Reader,

I have always been fascinated by the story of the Good Samaritan. It takes a lot of courage to stop and help a stranger, and it opens up the possibility of exposing your own life to others.

That's why I wrote this story. I got the idea from a newspaper article about a man who'd helped someone, then, because of all the attention, was forced to reveal certain aspects of his own less-than-perfect life. I thought it was sad that he'd stopped to help a fellow human being, but was now being persecuted for not being a perfect hero after all.

Derek Kane didn't want to be a hero; he just wanted to help others in need. Stephanie Maguire wanted a hero, but what she found was a real-life human being with flaws and misgivings. And she also found that she could love the man, not her image of what he should be.

In today's society, we focus a lot on images. It's good to take the time to focus instead on what really matters. Inner beauty, a solid faith, strength and integrity win out every time.

Until next time, may the angels watch over you while you sleep.

Lenora Worth

Take 2 inspirational love stories FREE!

PLUS get a FREE surprise gift!

Special Limited-Time Offer

Mail to Steeple Hill Reader Service™

In U.S.	In Canada
3010 Walden Ave.	P.O. Box 609
P.O. Box 1867	Fort Erie, Ontario
Buffalo, NY 14240-1867	L2A 5X3

YES! Please send me 2 free Love Inspired® novels and my free surprise gift. Then send me 3 brand-new novels every month, which I will receive months before they appear in bookstores. Bill me at the low price of $3.74 each in the U.S. and $3.96 each in Canada, plus 25¢ delivery and applicable sales tax, if any*. That's the complete price and a saving of over 10% off the cover prices—quite a bargain! I understand that accepting the books and gift places me under no obligation ever to buy any books. I can always return a shipment and cancel at any time. Even if I never buy another book from Steeple Hill, the 2 free books and the surprise gift are mine to keep forever.

303 IEN CM6R
103 IEN CM6Q

Name	(PLEASE PRINT)	
Address	Apt. No.	
City	State/Prov.	Zip/Postal Code

* Terms and prices are subject to change without notice. Sales tax applicable in New York. Canadian residents will be charged applicable provincial taxes and GST. All orders subject to approval. Offer limited to one per household.

INTLI-299   ©1998